The
Humble Lover

The Humble Lover

A Novel

Edmund White

BLOOMSBURY PUBLISHING

NEW YORK • LONDON • OXFORD • NEW DELHI • SYDNEY

BLOOMSBURY PUBLISHING
Bloomsbury Publishing Inc.
1385 Broadway, New York, NY 10018, USA

BLOOMSBURY, BLOOMSBURY PUBLISHING, and the Diana logo
are trademarks of Bloomsbury Publishing Plc

First published in the United States 2023

LIBRARY OF CONGRESS CATALOGING-IN-PUBLICATION DATA IS AVAILABLE

ISBN: HB: 978-1-63973-088-9; eBook: 978-1-63973-089-6

2 4 6 8 10 9 7 5 3 1

Typeset by Westchester Publishing Services
Printed and bound in the U.S.A.

To find out more about our authors and books visit
www.bloomsbury.com
and sign up for our newsletters.

Bloomsbury books may be purchased for business or promotional use. For
information on bulk purchases please contact Macmillan Corporate and
Premium Sales Department at specialmarkets@macmillan.com.

To Christopher Frizzelle

Losing above one's means . . .

—JOHN WIENERS, *Asylum Poems*

Love and sorrow walk hand in hand.

—CARL MARIA VON WEBER, *Der Freischütz*

I

He said to his very pale, very young companion, "It must be such a thrill to be a ballet dancer and have hundreds, thousands, of fans applauding you."

The young man, whose name was August Dupond, said dryly, "Yeah, I guess it is nice. A dream come true."

"Did you ever think you'd be a soloist in the greatest company in New York?"

The boy smiled weakly. "Well, that was the idea. Three classes every day for years, except for performance days, when I have only one afternoon class. Now or never, I guess." He smiled and took a sip of water. "Do you think they'd have Gatorade here?"

"What's that?"

"Gatorade. Oh, gosh, athletes drink it. Electrolytes."

"Gaston!"

"Yes, Monsieur West?"

"Monsieur Dupond would like a Gatra-Aid. I'll have a champagne cocktail. And the usual hors d'oeuvres."

August said hopefully, "A Gatorade?"

"I'm sorry, *jeune homme*, but I've never—"

"Is there a deli near here?"

"Not open, I fear."

"Skip it," August said with a tarnished smile. "Bring me a decaffeinated tea, please."

"*Tout de suite!*" the waiter said. He'd known Mr. West for nine or ten years and felt sorry that he was always accompanied by these underdressed youths who invariably ordered a hamburger or spaghetti, had strange food dislikes like mushrooms, and seldom would eat fish. One boy had asked him if the Dover sole was chicken.

"I'm so embarrassed they didn't have your health drink," Aldwych West said. He pulled out his agenda with its own gold pencil. "Here, if you'll just scribble the name of the drink I'll have a case delivered tomorrow."

"Why?"

"We might come back here some day. It's so close to the theater."

"*Le thé décaféiné pour le jeune monsieur. Et le champagne pour Monsieur West.*"

"*Merci.*"

"What language are you guys speaking?"

"French. Sorry. It must be very rude—"

"I thought it might be French. Real French. I'm French Canadian."

"Then you must understand—"

"No. Not really. We speak a funny French."

"They say that Canadian French is seventeenth-century French, the purest."

"*Joual.*"

"What's that?"

"I dunno. It's the name of our language, I guess. It's 'horse' in Canadian French—Oh, skip it."

Aldwych handed the black notebook with the gold-edged pages back to August, who just shrugged and pushed it away.

"Please . . ."

August blushed. Finally he said, "I don't know how to write it." He paused. "In school we studied real French. We don't write our *joual.* Maybe some people do. But it's not proper. It's not real French. In France they have to subtitle our movies."

"Of course," Aldwych said smoothly. "That's like Zurich, where they speak Schweizerdeutsch but the newspaper, *Neue Zürcher Zeitung,* is in real German."

"I wouldn't know. Oh, look, there's Zaza—you know her!" August sprang up and hurried over to an Asian girl who was dining with a much, much older white gentleman. The two old men studied each other disapprovingly and nodded politely. August pointed out Aldwych, and Zaza waved wildly with an enchanting smile.

When August finally came back, he said, "That man is Howard Marks."

"The dance critic?"

"Duh."

"Do you think I could send a bottle of champers to their table?"

"What?"

"Champagne? The Widow Clicquot?"

"She's got two performances tomorrow."

"Oh, yes, Saturday. Maybe the dessert wagon?"

"Dancers don't eat desserts."

"I'm learning so much from you."

"I think I really hurt my knee tonight." He pulled it up and nursed it with both hands. "I always suffer from those hops, I don't know why, it's just a *rond de jambe* and a little jump."

Aldwych passed the agenda toward him again, and, exasperated a bit (he was very polite), August said, "It's not important. And *grand ciel*, I'll never be able to spell '*rond de jambe.*'"

The older man was so charmed by the boy he was afraid he was grinning stupidly at him. He put a fat, beringed hand to his mouth and literally swept his smile away. Gaston (whose real name was Heinrich) brought the amuse-bouches out. August tried a tiny sausage wrapped in cooked dough but ate only half of it.

"And what would the messieurs desire for the *plat principal?*"

"Poutine," August said. When Gaston raised an eyebrow, August said, "Isn't that French? That's what we eat in Montreal. It's French fries—"

"*Pommes frites,*" Gaston said, "*d'accord,*" writing something down and nodding. "*Et ensuite?*"

"Cheese and gravy."

"Oh, no, monsieur, we can't make that. What about a nice am-bu-gaire?"

"Okay, fine, medium, no bun."

"*Une petite salade, peut-être?*"

"Okay, no dressing."

"*Et vous,* Monsieur West? Your usual *steak frites*? *Bleu*? And a glass of Bordeaux?"

After Gaston rushed away, Aldwych said, "We keep striking out."

August smiled. He had bad teeth. "You know, I think I'll run along. I'm exhausted." He pulled out his wallet and said, "What's my share?"

"Dear boy, nothing." And, a bit sad, he repeated, "Nothing."

. . .

Aldwych was vastly rich; his family had invented the microwave, or maybe something older, like the kitchen stove. They lived in Bernardsville, New Jersey, though neither Aldwych nor his sister Buffie had ridden with the very exclusive hunt club. She had made a debut, if reluctantly, and had run an unsuccessful art gallery in midtown till her death three years before; she'd never married. She'd shown a Morandi wannabe who didn't sell. Aldwych was the last of the line. He had an apartment in the East Sixties where he lived most of the time. He thought of writing a memoir titled *Alone with Servants*. He preferred the city to the country. He'd joined the Century Club because it was supposed to be artistic and lawyers weren't allowed to open their briefcases during lunch. You had to have eleven members recommend you in order to join. There were lots of lectures and concerts and a group dinner once a week—any member could come. And it was a good place for a pretheater dinner. On the parlor floor there was a good portrait of Henry James, young, with hair.

. . .

He attended the ballet every night, sat on the aisle in the tenth row with opera glasses. He was interested in the dancers, not the choreographers; he often read the paper during the Balanchines because that guy favored women over men. He couldn't tell why, since the men could leap higher. And oh, those butts! Ever since childhood he'd studied men's asses and crotches in black-and-white photos in *The Victor Book of Ballets*, though those dance belts squashed their manhood into anonymity. He'd looked for hours at Eglevsky's basket and was sure he could distinguish a certain swelling in there. The legs were powerful, of course, the forearms veined, the torso not much, the crack in the ass muscular and brilliant in those white tights. He wondered if he could buy a pair of used ballet slippers; they'd be so exciting to smell, lick, feel resting on his naked chest or stomach or face.

At first he was swept away in a delirium of male bodies, a crowd of muscle and a sea of sweat, but gradually he focused on one or two beauties, finally singling out August (originally Auguste, no doubt). He was dramatically pale, and rather small (which in Aldwych's occasionally—very occasionally—camp world was "bijou," as in "he's a total bijou"). As seen through the opera glasses, his eyes were blue, and the circles under them seemed to be where the color had faded and slipped. Aldwych studied the crotch to see if it moved or bulged; he excited himself by imagining the heat and moisture and density of that package (uncut, surely). Thankfully the boy's top was so tight you could see his heavy breathing ballooning his shirt after he'd engaged in a fury of *chaîné* turns and *tours jetés*. His upper body wasn't built up, but his visible breathing was a perfect gauge of his stamina. He didn't really sweat, the way children don't sweat. He looked too polar blue to sweat. Maybe Canadians didn't grow sweat glands—no need for them.

August had been promoted to the rank of *étoile* ten days after their dinner and could now take a solo bow. Aldwych arranged to have long-stemmed lilies or white roses in clear cellophane brought out to him by an usher at every curtain call, with his own name and phone number and a tiny "Bravo!" written clearly on the calling card. The overhead spotlights shattered across the cellophane. You could barely see the flowers. He knew the pursuit was hopeless, but he thought maybe the other dancers might notice and begin to tease him for having a secret admirer. They might scramble around him as he sat exhausted in the dressing room and open the small white envelope to read the name and say it out loud. Aldwych . . . Aldwych . . . Aldwych . . . Maybe they'd have trouble pronouncing the unfamiliar name and quiz each other on how to say it—anything to keep impressing his identity on the boy's mind. Of course August would never phone him, much less write him at his fancy address, but he might recognize the name if they were ever introduced.

Years ago he'd known Rebekah Harkness, who'd had her own ballet company. She was always a rebel. She'd dyed a neighbor's dog green, they said. She belonged to a noisy bitch squad of socialites who'd poured castor oil into the punch at parties. Aldwych had also known Bobby de Cuevas, whose father, a Chilean effeminate, had been married to an eccentric Rockefeller heiress. The interest on her stocks had financed his company, which collapsed with his death. Cuevas had bought his title in Spain. In Paris the name on his doorbell had said "M. Cuevas," then "M. de Cuevas," then finally "Marquis de Cuevas." Bobby, the son, was a nice chap who'd arrive at a party with a kilo of caviar.

Aldwych saw some old friends of his during the intermission, Mr. and Mrs. Phipps (he couldn't remember their Christian names); it turned out they were real balletomanes and worshipped Balanchine. They ranked him with Nabokov and Stravinsky, they said, as the Holy Trinity—white Russians who'd been refined by France and energized by America. "The three greatest artists of the twentieth century," she said. Aldwych thought she looked like Claude Picasso's ex-wife Sydney. Shouldn't Picasso be in that supergod bunch?

As they sipped their bad champagne during the intermission between *Prodigal Son* and *Agon*, the Phippses told him that they were friendly with the director of the company since they did some heavy-lifting fundraising for him. Thanks to Mr. Warburton, the finance officer, they'd met two of their favorite ballerinas, who'd even come to a benefit cocktail party at the Phippses' Fifth Avenue apartment, "across from the Metropolitan Museum." They'd become friendly with "Melissa" and "Tanny," especially Melissa, who'd met her third husband, a banker, through them—"an old classmate of Roger's from St. Paul's." Roger—that was his name! Roger Phipps.

During the extreme acrobatics and hard-on-the-ears Stravinsky score, Aldwych suddenly sat up straight, snatched out of his usual fog, and thought, *I must meet Mr. Warburton as well and make a major contribution to him in exchange for an introduction to August. Of course I cannot*

*make it too obvious. I'll get . . . Roger Phipps to counsel me
on the most discreet way to endow a chair in the orchestra or
something—an endowment "with benefits."* Aldwych actually
rubbed his hands together in delight and cornered the
Phippses at the next intermission, before *Stars and Stripes*,
in which August had a high-stepping solo. It was a fun,
patriotic ballet, and August was super-cute in his red
jacket with gold braid and blue tights. Aldwych was
besieged by a powerful daydream in which he slipped the
dresser five hundred bucks to steal those tights with their
funky butt-hole and stretched-out crotch and hand them
off in a brown paper bag to Aldwych at the stage door.
That night, after a final, consoling brandy, he looked in
the bathroom mirror at his shaggy, bulging body with
disgust, climbed the three mahogany steps into his
Virginia double bed (high enough for a slave to have slept
under it in the old days), and pulled back his luxurious
white Porthault sheets with the blue-scalloped pillow-
cases. *So much luxury,* he thought, *and all wasted on a lonely
man.* What would August think of his masculine rooms
with the hunting prints, dark green walls, and brass
fixtures? A youngster would scarcely notice the décor. He
thought he should throw it all out in the spring and start
with something new and austere; old people get used to
their surroundings and forget to refresh them.

   As he sank into sleep (he was breathing his own brandy
fumes ricocheting off a pillow that had rotated toward
him) he thought again of August's blue tights. In his

twilight sleep, he pulled the nylon fabric to his face and took in the layered odors of boy butt and cold lake (how did that get into the mix?). His dreams were all about not knowing the right platform and missing the train . . . again and again.

2

A few days later at one thirty, as he was about to go out to a ballet movie at the little cinema under Lincoln Center, he got a call from a Mr. Warburton, who identified himself as a vice president of the New York City Ballet.

"Oh, yes, I think Roger Phipps spoke of you."

"What a splendid chap!" Warburton exclaimed. He spoke with an upper-class English vocabulary and speech rhythms (incisive, then trailing off) but, oddly enough, not with an English accent. His sort of prissiness always pushed Aldwych toward sounding like a Midwestern hick and pronouncing "anyway" as "inny-way" rather than "ennuh-way."

"Yeah," Aldwych agreed, "great guy!" Then Aldwych explained that he was just rushing off to the Pina Bausch movie. They agreed to meet for a drink at four when the movie let out. "I'll be wearing an old-fashioned Chesterfield with a velvet collar," Aldwych said.

The film was strange because many members of the Wuppertal Dance Company had ordinary bodies, even ones perilously close to Aldwych's own. "Not my speed," he thought.

. . .

Mr. Warburton turned out to be a nice enough chap despite his grating English pretensions. He was portly, about fifty, liked his Scotch (some very expensive, unpronounceable Scots label), probably gay, which Aldwych divined from his affected speech, his impeccable shirt and tie combination despite the store-bought suit and worn-down heels, and his endless availability to donors, a freedom that suggested no wife, no children, no little hubby. He seemed to be a bachelor-who-loved-his-work, a type Aldwych had learned to avoid as bores.

After his third Laphroaig, Warburton did confess that dancers left him cold. "All that narcissism, all that white, white, sweated-through flesh that's never seen the sun or been exposed to raw air, the feeble arms and collapsed chests, the constant injuries and ACE bandages, the smell of VapoRub—Not My Cup of Tea, thank you very much!"

"That's strange, I'd think they'd present a constant temptation."

"Completely asexual—Bartender! One tiny more— They're always exhausted. And then those tiresome injuries and that blessed smell of camphorated unguents. Ugh! I prefer a thug from the Bronx, frankly. No, and they can't eat properly and they can't lie still, dancers. Utterly hopeless. And their heads may be pretty but they have no conversation except 'Dance, Dance, Dance, Little Lady'—we had that old seventy-eight record in the servants' quarters over the garage in Maine." He started singing in a surprisingly high voice, "Dance, dance, dance, little lady." He broke off and said, "Oh, yam filling veddy Gay tonight."

This confession led Aldwych to say he himself was not impervious to dancers' charms, not at all. And that he would become a $25,000 sponsor if he could hold a benefit for someone like, say—

"August?"

"Yes, that's amazing, how did you know?"

"He's the one most of 'em want. He does fill out that dance belt." He swallowed the rest of his shot and shook all over like a wet dog. "But I'm afraid only donors in the fifty thousand range can have a benefit with August."

Aldwych looked up sheepishly and asked, "Does he do many benefits in that range?"

"A few," Warburton said coolly.

"Well, I'd like to line him up. What is his availability?"

"I'm warning you, they come in pairs, like Mormon elders or nuns. He'll probably bring Zaza, the Asian girl he usually partners. She's small enough for him to lift; his arms are weak, though he's supposed to be working out with weights. And she doesn't tower over him even when she's *en pointe*."

"He's perfect," Aldwych sighed. Warburton shrugged. Aldwych had studied him through his opera glasses, after all.

"And they're not very good at circulating. They stick together and talk to each other about who's injured and who's learning the Glen Tetley role. But if your friends want to smile at real dancers from a distance and pay a thousand dollars each for the privilege and drink something white—vodka or white wine—so they won't stain the Aubusson . . ."

"I don't worry about the rug," Aldwych said grandly. "Give me two weeks and I'll round up twenty donors."

"Thirty? And don't expect the dancers to stay more than ten minutes. They don't eat or drink anything other than Gatorade. Of course we don't know their schedule, but once you settle on a day I'll organize them. You might send a car to pick them up. Oh, bartender?"

"A car, of course." His body, a little tired and a little drunk, settled into itself. Then he asked, jolting awake, "Say, Warburton, what do they get out of it?"

"You might get them a little gift from Tiffany's. Something silver—summer is coming up, after all." Warburton smiled a crooked smile. "And of course they'll get to meet their adoring fans."

"I'll make sure the Phippses are there." He couldn't think of any other ballet fans. Sailing, yes. Golfing, yes. Bridge, yes. Ballet, no.

Mr. Warburton said that he saw all the dancers every week because he was the bursar, the one who handed out their checks.

That night Aldwych put on his white cotton pajamas with the red piping and avoided the shaming bathroom mirror. He'd asked the maid to press his pajamas (and his underwear and his Porthault sheets). He knew that most Americans weren't that fussy, but he'd been spoiled by his years in Paris, just as the cook there had spoiled him by peeling his tomatoes.

A week later Warburton left a message on his answering machine (he didn't sound completely sober this time either). He gave a date when both Zaza and August would be available—"But they wanted to know if you were a nice guy."

Aldwych ordered from Tiffany tiny silver toe shoes for Zaza's charm bracelet (if she had one) and a silver ID bracelet for August (did guys even wear them now?). The invitation, provided by the ballet, said that guests could "mingle" with their favorite dancers for a mere thousand dollars and that the bar would be "open." Aldwych hired caterers and attractive "cater waiters" for the event and ordered cases of booze. He even engaged a harpist who brought her own instrument, helped by her gasping, chubby husband. She had to be banished to the second salon because her harp was too loud and interesting and upstaged the conversation. Everyone came except August; Zaza, in a severely tailored cream-colored suit, said he was resting after last night's premiere. He'd been slightly injured ("I think they make a mistake to have these teenagers jump so high and land on bones that aren't yet fully developed," she confided, though the boy seemed fully grown if slender. Aldwych was bitterly disappointed and had a terrible time. He was stuck with Zaza who under her thick makeup looked much, much older—thirty-two, he'd guess. The other forty guests brayed and swilled all night; they scarcely spoke to Zaza, though the Phippses grilled her on the upcoming premieres and cast lists.

And then suddenly he began to like Zaza. He gave her the tiny silver slippers and August's ID bracelet, which she promised to deliver. She was almost wet with gratitude, feigned or not. They were the two outsiders, though guest of honor and host. Almost no one came up to them, but gave them both a wide berth as if they were intimidating—as if the guests didn't want to be exposed as know-nothings. (Would Zaza grill them about what *en attitude* meant? *Ronds de jambe?*)

They were approached by a man who was overdressed with a gleaming rose-pink shirt that looked as if its matching foulard had been stitched to the shirt before being fluffed in an impressive Byronic knot meant to be read from the highest balcony. He was drunk and thought Zaza was in the Martha Graham company, which Aldwych imagined had been dissolved. "Frankly, if I can speak frankly, I had an affair with Martha. She was much older than me, of course." It was hard to conjecture how anyone could be older than the flamboyant gentleman.

Zaza murmured, "Of course. But how fascinating."

The gentleman said, "She thought of every man as a dildo."

"Even the gay ones?" Zaza asked.

"Of course not! A man is either straight or gay. Everyone knows that."

"Not in my world," Zaza said, and Aldwych suddenly wondered whether she and August might be lovers.

When the drunk man, indignant at the very idea of polyamory, staggered off for a refill, Zaza and Aldwych suddenly burst into laughter till they cried and begged each other to stop—"It hurts." "The poor man might think we're laughing at him," Aldwych said in a laugh-strangled voice as he doubled over and held his stomach. "We are!" cried Zaza, which only set off new agonies of hilarity. "Everyone knows that," Aldwych said, wiping his eyes.

When they finally calmed down, they each held up a hand like blinkers on a horse so they wouldn't see each other and start crying with laughter again. "Behave!" Zaza ordered.

She was so much fun, Aldwych thought. He blurted out: "Are you and August lovers?"

Zaza said blandly, "We tried once but we just fell asleep. I often sleep with him. He's afraid to sleep alone."

She grabbed a tissue and blew her nose. "I know you're in love with him," she added. "But I'm not sure he's ready for a lover his grandfather's age—"

"Of course not!"

"You might offer for him to come over after performances, though, and just sleep here. He's always looking for a sleeping companion."

"I don't snore!" Aldwych swore, though unbeknownst to him, he did.

He adored Zaza. "The only other Zaza I knew was Zsa Zsa Gabor. Though she wasn't very nice. That husband! And she'd lost both her legs somewhere." They both laughed cruelly. Then he said, "You're not bad, for a girl."

At that moment a balding redheaded man in his thirties with invisible eyelashes came up with a stylish wife wearing what looked like haute couture and enough jewelry for a rajah's wife.

"Oh, Bryce," Aldwych said. "And Ernestine." He kissed her hand as he'd been taught to do, without touching it.

"We wanted to see what all the merriment was about," Bryce said with a gentle smile. "We were tired of hearing about everyone's schedule. Have you noticed that people talk only about where they've been and where they're going?"

"This is Zaza. She's a ballet dancer—she's the guest of honor. And this is my nephew and his wife. In Paris I was taught you should give everyone a brief label, an *'etiquette.'* Bryce is an investment banker."

Ernestine, whose face reminded Aldwych of quilted steel, added, "And a philanthropist."

"Oh, really. Tell me, Bryce, what's your cause?"

"Restoring my wife's estate in New Jersey and opening it to the public one day a week."

Aldwych merely uttered that noncommittal "Mmm," the English murmur that can mean "yes" or "no" or "I wonder."

"But tell me," Bryce said, "what you two were guffawing over."

Aldwych said, bowing toward Zaza, "A lady never guffaws."

Ernestine said to Zaza, noticing her age under the spackling of her makeup, "And tell me, dear, have you been dancing long?"

"About twelve years, at first as a *coryphée*, then as an *étoile*, now as a *première danseuse*."

"Goodness," Ernestine said derisively. "And you, Uncle Aldwych? I never thought of you as having a charitable bone in your body. When I saw this invitation, Bryce can tell you how astonished I was." She hooked a thin, bluish arm, weighted by its diamonds, through her husband's richly upholstered one. Aldwych rather despised them.

Bryce and Ernestine left for more Roederer and foie gras.

"I don't want to sound too pushy," Aldwych said, "but if I wanted to invite August for a sleepover, how would I contact him?" He imagined he was blushing and touched his face to see if it was hot. It wasn't.

"Just call him," Zaza said. "Here's his number." Aldwych produced his agenda with its gold pencil and she wrote the number down. "Cell number. Start out with dinner; it might startle him if you suggest bed right away." She twinkled. He liked her immensely.

That's how he ended up with August at Boulud's the night they'd seen Zaza with the dance critic—the night August had skipped out on him.

. . .

He called August again two days later. "Zaza says you hate sleeping alone. Would you like to come here and sleep with me, just sleep? I could leave a peanut butter and grape jelly sandwich for you. I know you'll be exhausted after dancing *Four Temperaments*. I could have my car waiting for you out front with your name in the window. You wouldn't have to talk to me or anything. In fact we'll have a rule of silence."

"Okay, but I hate peanut butter. As a child I had very big tonsils and it got stuck in my throat."

"Tuna fish? Chicken?"

"Chicken and mayonnaise."

Aldwych heard him come in, piss, go into the kitchen for his sandwich and a glass of milk, then come into the bedroom, where Aldwych pretended to be asleep beside a dim light. He had never been so thrilled in his life. He heard the boy step out of his trousers; the belt buckle tapped the parquet floor. He took off his shirt audibly and folded it neatly on a chair. He kept his under-pants on. He climbed into the bed and weighted it so little the mattress didn't budge in his direction. A moment later he was asleep and breathing heavily. Aldwych wept with joy till dawn.

3

As they took off their outerwear, Bryce asked, "Did you have fun? I'm sure you didn't."

Ernestine said, "I was never so bored."

"You don't even like ballet, do you?"

"Can't bear it. All that sweat and clobbering around on bleeding toes. Anyway, what's your uncle doing with that . . . Asian . . . ballerina? I thought he was gay."

"He is. But the poor thing has been in the closet his whole life, even married, though everyone assumes he's gay. Whiskey?"

"Open the bottle of Montrachet."

"All right." It took him a few minutes in the kitchen and six "Damns!" to find the corkscrew. " Maybe he's taken up with women."

"Hmm."

"Maybe the lioness is changing her spots," Bryce said.

"Oh, my darling, humor is not your strong suit. There has to be a dirty little boy somewhere in the mix to interest Aldwych." She violently twisted Bryce's nipples. He shouted and spilled some of the wine. "You know you love it. Your uncle thinks we're so dull and normal, but I stupefied him tonight telling him your nipples are larger than mine."

"You didn't! You told him that?"

She didn't answer but sat low in a chair and extended a foot toward him. She growled, "Take off my boot."

For a moment he looked dubious, as if it were up to him, then sank into a boneless puddle on the floor, took her foot very professionally into his hands, unlaced the boot, pulled it off, rolled down the stocking, and deliriously inhaled the warm flesh before rousing himself and unshodding the other foot. His wife lit a cigarette and scooted down further. He went to work bathing each foot with his tongue, not neglecting the delicious spaces between the toes. She tapped her ash onto his combover.

She remembered after a basketball game how Sister Marie-Thérèse wanted her, as her favorite prefect, to massage her feet and how the older woman had finally, on the third occasion, rolled down her black stockings and surrendered her tiny toes and high insteps and thick, pale, hairless ankles to little Ernestine's busy hands and at last to her even busier tongue. The nun's body, under its copious black robes smelling of adult woman, had stretched and buckled, and to stifle her moans, she'd put

uncircumcised penis and heavy balls, those genitalia
Aldwych had offered ten thousand dollars for and had
actually engulfed for seventy-five. Now that they were
on display and unmysterious, they seemed unobtainable
at any price. The contract between them had slipped into
friendship.

"But how did it happen that you were penniless on
Third Avenue?"

"I lied." August smiled but kept his teeth hidden by
his long upper lip. "I never took lessons from a Russian
lady in our Canadian village."

"Really?"

"No, at fourteen I ran away from my parents and ended
up in Montreal in the gay neighborhood, Sainte-
Catherine. There were lots of go-go bars there. For a
really big tip—twenty-five Canadian—you'd go into
a booth with an American tourist and fuck him. There was
a strip club, Campus, for really young twinks. Gay porn
on the TVs. Lots of naked boys. Open till three A.M. Very
very loud. Anyway, a retired dancer from ABT—I won't
say his name—*un mec* who retired twenty years ago and
now teaches—he liked my moves on the stage and stayed
till closing time. He took me out for a poutine dinner in
a Celine Dion restaurant, the only one that stays open
late, and then he invited me back to his very nice hotel
room and fucked me with his big dick in every position.
He didn't even mind that my hole was dirty, he said
'We're all human.' Of course I was so tired from drinking

and drugging and dancing all night that I passed out, but when I came to half an hour later he was still plowing my butt. It felt good and I must have fallen asleep again. The next day he told me that I was the best fuck of his life and that he'd loved it when I passed out and just surrendered my young tight hole to him. He was from Texas and said, 'I turned you every which way but loose.' I'd kept his babies in me all night and I shat out lots of come and some blood the next morning. He ordered us pancakes when we got up. He wheeled the room service table out into the hall, put up the Do Not Disturb sign, and was fucking me again—twice! I know how everyone now talks about predators and I was only fourteen and he was forty-two, but people forget how kids like me, runaways, are so grateful to johns who feed us and let us shower and sleep in clean sheets and kiss us and fuck our holes and maybe give us a few bucks, it seems a fair exchange. He was better than that. He drove me over the border in his Honda Accord into the States at an unguarded place he knew of and kept me with him in his Hell's Kitchen apartment and even bought me some clothes and took me with him to a dance class he was teaching in jazz/modern and I caught on very quickly. I learned to cook for him and how to stay out of his way when he was in a mood. When the other students asked me where I'd learned to dance so well I made up that story about the Russian teacher in our village and the Montreal Ballet. He liked to have three-ways and watch some top fuck me. He didn't have a sense of humor but he was nice, usually."

Do I have a sense of humor? Aldwych wondered.

"So I'm sorry I lied to you, Aldwych, and I've felt very guilty about it."

"Don't worry, August." He got up to put the plates and cutlery into the dishwasher. "What do you want from me?"

August frowned and asked, "What do you mean?"

"How do you want me to be around you?"

August smiled. "Love me a little bit less but love me a long time." He looked away. "That's my favorite line from a French movie."

6

Aldwych was suddenly embarrassed about how empty his days were compared to August's, who was busy some performance days for eleven hours straight.

"Don't you ever get exhausted? Or rebellious?"

"Never. Our careers are so short. I'm so grateful to be making art with my body."

"Aren't you worried about your future?"

August patted Aldwych's liver-spotted hand. "Everyone asks the same questions. Are you anorexic? Do you ever have fun? Sex? Read a book? Aren't you in constant pain? Do your feet bleed? Don't all dancers end up crippled and suicidal at forty? Have you put any money aside? Will anyone know your name a year after your retirement?"

Aldwych looked at his fat hand and somehow blamed it for all the stupid questions, which he in fact had entertained. "What do you say in response?"

"I just look at them in pity because I suspect they've never known the hard-won ecstasy a dancer knows. Maybe in sex with drugs, maybe at the altar after days of fasting, maybe in a convertible racing next to the sea at midnight—who knows? But a dancer can count on ecstasy seven performances a week. I never feel so free as when I'm dancing—all my problems melt away."

"Seven?"

"Don't forget the Saturday matinee. They usually schedule us for a day off, each of us principals."

"I never heard you so eloquent."

"Really? It's fun talking to you."

"Likewise. Why don't you move in? I could give you your own bedroom, bathroom, and sitting room. Would you like to see them?"

"Sure."

"No strings attached."

They were walking down the long dark hall. Aldwych snapped on a faint overhead light cupped inside a Lalique flower. "You would have full kitchen privileges, of course."

"What if I brought a guy over for sex?"

"That wouldn't bother me."

"Really?"

"Absolutely not, "Aldwych swore bravely. "It would just be fun having you around. And if your bed was empty and you were scared or something, you could climb in with me—"

"Not scared. I'm never scared. It's just that my mind races. I keep going over the new choreography. I keep saying to myself 'Battement, avant, derrière, attitude, arabesque two three, passé, fourth position,' that kind of rubbish."

"Not rubbish. That's your work. It's like competing in the Olympics."

"No, if athletes do something beautiful it's almost by accident, but we aim at beauty every moment. The port de bras, our arm gestures, our rhythms and movements bound to the music, our constant smiles unless poker faces are called for. Our long lines—that's why we're supposed to have slender bodies, long necks, small heads. Our répétiteur says the head must follow through, must brilliantly snap into place, eyes on the horizon, that the head and its tilt is the most important part of the dancer's body. He's a funny old thing, fake blond, always in white, makes the students wear black—and such a big hungry butt. They say that's why you see so few black dancers—their butts are too big. Pretty absurd, if you think of the Dance Theatre of Harlem or José Limón or Alvin Ailey's company or the great Balanchine dancer Arthur Mitchell. Girls who have fat legs are out, or if they're too busty. It's weird, but we're so busy our friends are usually the other dancers, but they're also our biggest competitors. We all want the same thing. The other guys are always friendly and, since they're Americans, mostly joking around. Americans are always joking. I've done class in Europe when we're touring and there they are more formal, which in a way is less hypocritical. Each dancer is a tidy, little unit in Paris or Berlin, and the longest conversation is about which metro to take or where to buy slippers. The French are always 'correct,' though they find my accent absurd, even our vocabulary. I remember asking a completely puzzled French guy where the nearest *dépanneur* was, which in Canada means a deli but in France means a car repair. And the French call an automobile *une voiture* and we call it *un char*, which in real French means a chariot or a cart at the supermarket. Wow! This room is great! And here's another room. But I could never afford two rooms of my own in Manhattan! This must be eight thousand a month."

"Hush! It's nothing for you. Even the maintenance is miniscule. I own this place. See—it has an air conditioner. I won't come back here unless you invite me. The maid, Rosita, will change your sheets and towel once a week— make that two towels, in case you have a guest."

"I won't. I haven't had sex in a month. I'm always too tired. But the good thing about sex is it's always a possibility, isn't it? Isn't this nice? You won't spoil everything by falling in love with me, will you?"

"Of course not," Aldwych lied. The lover doesn't want to have sex all the time with the beloved as long as the beloved has sex with no one else. "We're just friends. Best friends."

"You're the perfect friend. No one will believe that a twenty-year-old boy is just friends with—How old are you?"

"Seventy-nine."

"With a seventy-nine-year-old man. Everyone will think you're keeping me."

"We'll know better. You'll be completely independent."

"If my mother comes to New York to see me dance, can I put her up here? I don't want to install her in a hotel. It would only confuse her at her age."

"Of course you can. How old is she?"

"Almost forty. But a bad, cranky, bigoted forty, though very dear. I can sleep with you."

"Won't that be awkward?"

"No, we only have two big beds and a couch at home. We all double up. We're eight kids."

"I see," Aldwych said, feeling like an idiot. Should he be astonished or act as if it was normal, such poverty?

"I'm sure you don't see, "August said with a laugh. "By the way, August Dupond is my stage name. My real name is Eddie Vielleville, but that sounded too much like Eddie Villella, so I changed it. My mother is Marthe Vielleville. Don't be surprised when my mother calls me Eddie."

"By the way, Rosita will wash and iron your shirts. Just leave them here." Aldwych opened the closet and held up a muslin drawstring bag.

"I wouldn't want to bother her—"

"That's her job. She's here five days a week for four hours every day and hates to be idle. She's Panamanian. Perfectly legal. American husband. She's an American citizen. I pay money for her into Social Security and I'm building up a generous retirement fund. Her daughter helps out when we have guests."

"When I'm old and hobbling maybe I could work for you too? Oh—I've got class in an hour. I'm not performing tonight, but Jorge, the ballet master, is working with me on the Apollo variation, which I'm going to dance next week if all goes well. Maybe tonight we can watch Baryshnikov dance it on YouTube?"

"Why not bring Zaza? We'll order in some Chinese."

"She's off someplace in the country. Just you and me tonight."

They watched Baryshnikov ten times in a row, and Rosita had prepared lamb chops with cumin and five kinds of cooked vegetables, no sauce, no butter. They were very cozy, but there was no talk except August's comments: "I like the way he just walks around normally and then looks astonished to discover his lute on the ground, picks it up with his hands crossed so that when they're lifted and reversed to play they're in the right position to strum and fret. Did you notice how when he first plays the lute he winds up his arm like a baseball pitcher?"

Later August laid his head on Aldwych's shoulder and said, "I love this music." It was for Apollo's apotheosis. "Any other composer and it would sound like movie music."

Aldwych felt inferior to his young friend, who was so much smarter, whose mind was so restless. Aldwych was grateful he was rich; at least he had something to offer. "Would you like your teeth to be capped?"

August clapped a hand to his mouth. "Aren't they horrible?"

Aldwych grinned and said, "Mine are capped."

"Does it hurt?"

"Novocaine. It's just sort of tedious. They have to drill down your real teeth so they can put a bridge over them."

"Ça coûte cher?"

"It's worth it. A beautiful face should have a beautiful smile. It will be your birthday present. August is coming up."

"You can't imagine how much I suffer from my horrible teeth. They show how poor my family was. Poor people have bad teeth. I can never smile. That's why people think I'm cold. Most dancers are from bourgeois families."

"But none of them is as beautiful or as talented as you are." Although Aldwych felt very daring saying that, he realized August scarcely took it in. To the boy's mind the older man was just a flatterer and in love. Aldwych's opinion didn't count. Back to practicalities: "They'll take impressions of your teeth. A surgeon will remove the broken and dead ones. They'll put in temporary plastic teeth while your gums are healing. A month later they'll put in the new ones; you'll look like a movie star."

"But what can I do for you in return?"

"Just be. Just dance. Just share my life, at least once in a while."

"I know—I'll give you tokens, each worth an hour of my time. I'll do chores for you."

"You have everything except free time. In fact, we'll have trouble finding free hours for the dentist, given your schedule."

"Do you like massages? I give good ones."

"No. If we were in the Middle Ages I'd ask you to wear my colors."

"I'd be your knight," August said with a smile.

The boy is frightfully clever, Aldwych thought. *I was a dunce at his age. I flunked out of three prep schools. I'm still a dunce.*

7

A week later Ernestine came to Aldwych's aisle seat a few minutes before the first ballet began. "Where have you been, Aldwych dear? We've been emailing you like crazy and leaving messages on your cell and landline, but we've been drawing blanks."

"You look very nice, Ernestine. New haircut? Is Bryce here this evening?"

"Oh, dear, the orchestra is tuning up. I must scurry."

"I'll see you at the little bar on this floor at the intermission?"

"You better make it good."

His elderly seat partner said, "Your daughter?"

"No, another nephew. His wife."

She raised her eyebrows at the thought of a heterosexual "nephew" and touched her hearing aid as if she'd misheard. "And your other nephew? Is he dancing tonight?"

"Yes, Apollo."

"What?"

"Apollon musagète."

She nodded vaguely and whispered something to her companion.

August was magnificent, at once athletic and godlike, and Zaza, who was dancing Terpsichore for the first time, seemed very assured. Aldwych knew that after he spun into the wings they clapped an oxygen mask to his face for a moment and pushed him back onstage. The crowd went wild for August during his one solo bow; tonight's flowers were white roses. Aldwych wondered if he should go home before *Who Cares?*, which August wasn't dancing, of course. Would August already be home? Or would he stay to celebrate? If he left now, Ernestine wouldn't have a chance to grill him. But she trapped him just as he was sneaking out with his Burberry and cashmere cap on. "Aldwych!" she shouted. Bryce was standing beside her, looking smaller and more sheepish than usual, grinning as if he'd just eaten something delicious he knew was bad for his heart. Aldwych turned back and smiled, joined them for an instant.

"Wasn't August *mah*velous!"

"Yes, marvelous."

"I'm surprised you're not going backstage to congratulate him."

"Actually, August is living with me." He said it to stun her into silence; he was proud of the connection, but he regretted sharing information with her, the hag.

She made a quick recovery. "What's it like to live with a god, with Apollo?"

"He's a lot of fun," Aldwych said in a deliberately bored voice.

Ernestine raised an eyebrow and said, "I imagine."

"No, it's perfectly innocent. I give him a break on the rent."

"From your lips to God's ears, or a god's ears."

Aldwych blew them a kiss and took off. August was at home in Aldwych's silk Lanvin wrapper. He was watching TV and eating some of Rosita's beef stew he'd warmed up.

"You were brilliant tonight!" Aldwych exclaimed.

August looked up with a tear-stained face. "You can't imagine what the other boys were saying just on the other side of the stage curtain while I was taking my bows. They all noticed how I stumbled going up those stairs at the end, before the girls join me for the final tableau."

Aldwych sat down beside the boy and grabbed his shoulder. "Those evil bitches! Unfortunately you'll have to get used to that now you're a star. They're just jealous."

After another moment of brooding, August looked up with a sudden smile and said, "A scout from the San Fran- cisco Ballet, a scout or someone—" he crossed the room to look into his trouser pockets and pulled out the man's card. "No, he's the ballet master, it says. Anyway, he asked if I'd dance Apollo out there for three performances."

Aldwych's heart sank—this was the price of stardom. "Can I ask you a question? Will you be honest?"

Oh, dear, Aldwych thought. "Of course."

"Does my breath stink? With all my rotten teeth?"

"Honestly . . . it does. But I've become intoxicated by it. I try to get a whiff of it when you're asleep."

"Eeww!"

"You said I should be honest. A classmate of mine at St. Paul's fought in Korea afterward and he told me he fell in love with a whore who was always eating kimchi— fermented cabbage, you know?—and he'd get a hard-on the instant he smelled that smell. Even the smell of bad teeth can become intoxicating. Anyway, soon you'll have all new teeth."

"Not a minute too soon," August said. "Someone from the *New Yorker* is interviewing me tomorrow. Luckily it will be over the phone." He blew into his cupped hand. "Poor you, sleeping with my rancid mouth-hole."

"I'm the most honored man in the world. I love everything about you."

"I adore you." He bit his lip. "But just as a friend, you know."

"I know that. I respect your boundaries," he lied.

The ballet went to Saratoga for their summer season, and Aldwych rented a four-bedroom house on the lake with a dock and a hot tub and (the notice said) Amish furniture and a fire pit, whatever they were. August objected to the "extravagance" and suggested it might look funny to the other dancers in such a small town to be shadowed by his rich grandfather (his *"oncle d'Amérique,"* as the French said). Anyway, August said, the company had arranged accommodations for all the dancers, and he wanted to be part of the gang.

Aldwych humbly and coolly replied that he usually went somewhere in the summer, often in Provence, but he'd found Saint-Rémy too hot and the cicadas maddening, those little Bacchantes, and he liked the idea of being beside a freshwater lake.

"The mosquitoes are worse than the cicadas," August observed. Aldwych could see August was definitely feeling crowded and decided to let the subject drop. But the older man went silently forward with his summer plans. When August brought it up again, Aldwych said, "I've decided to have our place here steam-cleaned and redecorated while we're both away. Do you have any preferences as to how the apartment should look? Your rooms? Traditional? The Rothschild style?"—by which he meant pattern on pattern, fringe on the lampshades, a mixture of periods, an aesthete's hodgepodge. "Classical with Pompeii frescoes? California with Diebenkorns and blue-and-white-striped fabrics?"

"Don't waste your money on that. Everything looks fine as it is."

That was exactly what Aldwych thought, but he'd wanted to give August lots of options. He knew that August was used to living in rented rooms and hotels and didn't even notice his surroundings—he just wanted a place to shower and sleep and boil an egg. "If you ever want someone to sleep with in Saratoga, I'll be there. Or if you want me to organize a swim party and barbecue for the cast, with or without my presence, remember the house is at your disposal."

"That's a great idea. But how would I explain it to the others?"

"Board member of the ballet."

"*Zut*, you've thought of everything." He slipped in a breath freshener and gave Aldwych a kiss on his head. Aldwych wanted to say that there was no reason to worry about his breath around him, but he feared bringing up the delicate subject again.

One night August returned with a young man (Aldwych was already in bed watching Classic Arts Show-case on the City University of New York channel—it must have been late, since the program didn't even start until one in the morning). They were obviously drunk and laughing and stumbling down the hall—Oops! It sounded as if they'd just knocked one of the Japanese prints off the wall. That accident provoked another squall of laughter, two young male voices tumbling out one over the other. Then they slammed shut the hallway door leading into August's rooms. Aldwych was tempted to tiptoe down the hall and eavesdrop, but he was afraid one of them might burst through the door in search of a beer or a glass of water. Even from the sitting room he could hear their voices, or rather August's. He was groaning with pleasure. Aldwych could even hear words: "My God . . . that's the biggest . . . Oh, God, that feels good." It was August's voice, he was sure. Then the other guy must have really started fucking August hard because the bedstead was knocking rhythmically and quickly against the wall. It went on and on. Half an hour. Forty-five minutes. The doorbell rang. Aldwych put on his robe and answered. It was the landlady, cold-creamed and indignant, her hair in giant curlers. Her eight rooms were just below his eight. "Mister West, are you building something at this hour? My bedroom is just below where you're working."

"I'm so sorry, Mrs. Greenville, I couldn't sleep. I was stacking the books I want to sell in my spare room. I had no idea your bedroom was just below. I'm terribly sorry."

"I suggest you pile books at an earlier hour." As she walked back toward the elevator she called over her shoulder, "I heard shouts and screams as well. I was afraid someone was hurting you or you were having a medical incident. A stroke."

As soon as Aldwych locked up, he went back to August's door and knocked timidly. August was naked, his penis half hard, a big boyish grin on his face. He and his companion—he looked vaguely Mexican to Aldwych—were both grinning, and the room was heavy with marijuana smoke. Aldwych was introduced to Pablo, who said to August, "I thought you said this was your *aunt's* place."

"He's my uncle."

Aldwych explained the landlady problem and told them they were welcome to use his bed.

"No, dude, we done finished. Your nephew's got quite the ass, mister."

"He should. He spends hours exercising it."

"Awesome."

They were both stoned, utterly unselfconscious about their nudity and affectionate as puppies. They walked in all their splendid physicality into the living room, arms around each other, then sat on either side of Aldwych on the couch. They wanted orange juice; luckily there was a half gallon in the fridge.

"Have you ever seen such a big dick?" August held it up and smiled innocently at Aldwych.

"It is very big."

"It felt wonderful in me," August said, as if he were reporting on a massage to the man who'd paid for it.

"You're both beautiful boys, "Aldwych said, placing the palm of his white, liver-spotted hand on Pablo's knee, which was nearly black in the half-light and evenly flecked with tiny, even blacker hairs no bigger than the brushstrokes in a Seurat (he owned one, which he kept in the vault: a boy in a hat playing a flute).

"It gets even bigger when it's hard."

Pablo said, "Are we embarrassing you, mister? Maybe you want a blunt?"

"Not at all. Would you like some vodka in your orange juice?"

"*Claro*," Pablo said, which Aldwych took to mean yes. He found a bottle and poured a heavy shot into each glass.

August had slipped to the floor, kneeling between Pablo's legs. He said, "Gross, your dick tastes of my ass."

Pablo scooted further down and opened his legs and closed his eyes. "You love to taste it," he said. "*Bueno, bueno.*"

August sucked faster and faster. Aldwych kneeled behind August and inserted two fingers into his ass. He loved the feel of the hot lubricated hole pulsing on his finger. Aldwych wrapped his other hand around and began to stroke August's erection. He'd heard gays talk about "spit-roasting"; he was sure this wasn't what they meant, but nonetheless he said to himself, *I'm spit-roasting August.*

Pablo shouted "Ay!" as he came all over August's face. August pushed Aldwych's hand away to jerk himself off faster to a climax, and Aldwych licked the ejaculate clean. Then, knowing from experience how a climax could shift the filter from a becoming pink to a harsh white, could arouse disgust and repentance in a man who'd been a single-minded horndog a second earlier, Aldwych vanished into his shower, dried himself off, and slipped back into his bed. The boys giggled and mumbled for a few more minutes in the living room, then Pablo must have dressed and left. August crept into his bed.

"Are you mad?"

"No. Are you?"

August was silent for a moment and sighed, "That was hot."

Aldwych said, "Very. Where did you meet Pablo?"

"I know these drags who came to the show and I went with them to the Industry Bar in Hell's Kitchen and then to Therapy. That's where I met Pablo. He came on strong. He was drunk or high. Did you ever see a guy that hung?"

"No. Never. You should invite him to Saratoga Springs."

A moment later August was asleep, and Aldwych pushed the pillow out of the way so he could inhale his foul, endearing breath. He almost purred when he remembered he'd fingered the best ass in New York.

The next morning he sent a dozen roses to Mrs. Greenville with a note reading "You'll be happy to hear Books has moved on."

8

He invited Zaza and Pablo and Ernestine and August to lunch. It had to be at three, since the dancers had rehearsals till then. Mrs. Rothkopf made a lovely salad with avocados and tiny shrimp and some finely chopped fennel with just a soupçon of vinaigrette, then she gave everyone just a half of a Guinea hen with a stuffing of Israeli couscous, apricots, chopped onion, and grated lemon peel. And a baked apple for dessert. She had Gatorade to drink, which she disguised with sprigs of mint, and for the non-dancers some Gewürztraminer. Rosita served. In the sitting room there were espresso, tisane in a thermos, and a plate of macaroons of every color.

Ernestine asked if it was true that the répétiteur was very harsh and hit them with a stick. Zaza laughed and said, "No sticks. I think that went out a hundred years ago. But they can be harsh if you can't get your leg up really high or if you simplify a three-part step to two. Or if you've gained a pound. They'll pinch your waist. They're fanatics about preserving Balanchine's choreography. All of the dances were filmed under Balanchine's supervision. Of course it's all built on the classical ballet technique, but in the Stravinskys or the Hindemith or in Jerry's *The Cage*—"

"Also a Stravinsky score," August added.

"In those ballets, the hand gestures are new, entirely new, the rhythms syncopated, even the steps distorted sometimes . . ."

"My goodness," Ernestine said condescendingly, "you people are so cultured."

"Only about dance," August said. "We don't know anything else."

"Oh, my darlings, you're too, too modest," Ernestine protested.

When Ernestine asked, Pablo said he repaired bicycles and lived at home in Crown Heights. Somewhat fatuously Ernestine said, "Bicycles? How lovely. I have a bicycle." Later she asked if Crown Heights was in New York. He didn't seem to know how to hold a fork or how to shift it to his right hand for eating. He kept his head down, and August played with his leg under the table. Pablo smiled cryptically.

"And you, Zaza? Where are you from?"

"Oakland."

"No," Ernestine pursued. "I mean *originally*."

"My parents are from the Philippines."

"Oh, like Imelda! I knew her. Terrible bore." Then she said, "The Philippines. They're on my bucket list."

Zaza was a little vexed and asked, "Where are you from *originally?*"

Ernestine looked startled. "Me? I'm American. From Georgia. My ancestors? Oh, they've been here for centuries. England, I suppose, Scotland, Ireland. All poor farmers in Virginia. They signed their wills with an X."

"Did they have many slaves?" Zaza asked inconveniently.

"I suppose. They raised cotton. Why do you ask?"

"No reason," Zaza said sweetly.

Ernestine thought it was hard to find a general subject with poor people. You couldn't ask them for their itineraries because they didn't go anywhere. As Fran Liebowitz said once, "They summer where they winter." Nor could they complain about their parents' cute little foibles, since their parents were brutal or alcoholic or absent or exhausted. They couldn't complain about their "staff," since they didn't have any. August seemed ashamed of his family. Ernestine wondered how they earned a living up in the snow country of Quebec—did they collect maple syrup in little tin pails? Or just live off the dole and watch TV? In French? Pablo was very sexy, and Ernestine assumed that was why he was invited—but it was hard to have a conversation with a penis. Even a large Mexican penis. Was everyone a foreigner these days? Ernestine wondered why *she* had been invited. She did enjoy looking at August. But if he wasn't going to sleep with her, what good was he? She asked herself if he were bisexual. He was certainly a vastly talented creature—though that mouth! those black teeth!—and he obviously had a sense of humor. As for Aldwych, he was old, inadequate, and familiar. Absolutely no mystery there! No wonder he was attracted to this wunderkind, this bbb (beautiful ballet boy)!

In overlapping voices, Zaza and August described their upcoming tours. First Europe: Covent Garden, the Paris Opéra, three days in Munich, a week in Berlin, a week at La Scala. Then Asia—San Francisco and L.A. on the way, then Tokyo, Peking, Shanghai, Taipei (two nights). Before the Christmas season of *The Nutcracker* they'd have three weeks in New York to learn new ballets for the January–February season.

"My gosh, don't you ever get a rest?" Ernestine asked. She was playing with the jade elephant on her bracelet.

Zaza said, "We're not like actors or singers who can study a script or a score with a vocal coach between engagements. If we're not dancing almost every day with the company, we fall apart. That's why we tour the world and feel lucky to be doing so. And our reviews in England, Paris, and Italy keep reestablishing the prestige of the New York City Ballet in America; it reassures our board and the trustees."

"Surely they're way beyond that!"

Zaza said, "Are you kidding? Anything can spook them. And though we have our warhorses—*The Nutcracker*, *A Midsummer Night's Dream*—many of our ballets are new. There's one by Justin Peck to a score by Nico Muhly—"

"Who?"

"Exactly. See the problem? If we just recycled our old hits we'd actually make a profit. As it is we're running to seventy percent capacity."

Ernestine smiled. "You've got a very good head for business."

Zaza asked, "Where is your husband?"

"He didn't want to come."

"Why not?"

"He claims he was abused as a child by Aldwych's older brother."

Aldwych said, "That's outrageous. He actually *said* that?"

"Only to me."

"But it can't be true."

"It probably is true, but so what? Your brother is a horny bastard with his five marriages and endless paternity suits. I'm sure he buggered Bryce—but only in retrospect is that *abuse*. That's so modish to claim now. Surely he fucked you too?"

Aldwych blushed and looked at his plate.

"*Ennuh*way, that's why Bryce avoids you. He thinks you're abusing August and he doesn't want to be any part of it."

August fell into her trap. "Aldwych and I have never had sex! We're just dear friends—can no one understand that? Does everyone think I'm cynical, that darling Aldwych is cynical?"

Ernestine drank the dregs of her cold espresso. "You have to admit it looks fishy."

August's voice went up an octave and his French accent reemerged in the emphasis of certain syllables and in his way of saying "dat" for "that." "Dat is complete*lee* cura*zee*! We gist luff each uzzer."

Aldwych wasn't sure if he wanted to be loved if that meant everyone knew they weren't having sex.

"Anyway it is not *abuze*, I am an *addoolt*."

Aldwych said, "Anyway it's silly to blame me for something my brother might or might not have done in the mists of time. And my relationship with August is not something for Bryce to approve of or not."

Ernestine seemed pleased by the ruckus she'd raised. "Well, I'm just telling you why he's not here."

"He's welcome to his embargo," Aldwych said.

Ernestine was worried about the inheritance now. "I told him he was exaggerating and that his uncle's private life was none of his business."

Aldwych chuckled. "Apparently I don't have a private life."

Ernestine thought, *Like uncle, like nephew, no sense of humor.*

Pablo had begun to play with August's crotch under the tablecloth and was twisted with laughter, the more so as August, with a pained smile, tried to return his hands to his lap. Instead of blushing, August went even paler until his eyes were just bullet holes in a sheet. He stood to escape Pablo's devilish hands, but he was half erect, which Ernestine took in appreciatively.

"I'm going to take a nap, as I always do after class. It was wonderful to see you, Ernestine." He kissed her on one cheek as New Yorkers do and then pulled a giggling Pablo down the hall.

When they were alone, Ernestine jerked her head toward the boys, who were roughhousing their way to August's door, and whispered, "Does that torment you, Aldwych?"

"Not at all, "Aldwych said in a loud, toneless voice. "Young men need their outlets."

Ernestine sat back down on the edge of her seat. "I sometimes wonder if August is even gay. Really gay. Deeply."

They both looked at Zaza, who averted her eyes and shrugged. Then, with a new spurt of enthusiasm, Zaza looked at Aldwych: "Don't take Pablo seriously. He'll be gone in a week. Dancers don't make good lovers—always exhausted. Always in pain. *You* are essential to August."

Ernestine asked, "Did he tell you that in so many words?"

"Yes."

The two women left together. On their way out, Aldwych asked Ernestine, "Does your husband really think I abuse August? Does he really dislike my brother for supposedly abusing him, whatever that means between twelve-year-olds?"

Ernestine replied "He has too much time on his hands" and kissed Aldwych on his cheek.

Both women thanked Aldwych for the lovely luncheon.

Aldwych could smell the marijuana smoke in the hallway. It didn't displease him that August felt free to pursue his adventures here. All sex should be kept under his roof.

9

The boys came out again in the nude, their bodies gleaming with lubricant and smelling of manure, their manner bleached clean and innocent by the marijuana. They were like big babies, smiling and uncomprehending. They sat once again on the couch on either side of Aldwych, who was smiling with more intention, a greater awareness, grateful that this was the maid's day off.

Pablo stood beside Aldwych, a little too close. "Go on. Touch it. You know you want to."

Aldwych looked at August, who said, "Leave the poor guy alone."

Pablo dressed and left, blowing silly, ironic kisses.

When August, still very stoned, came back and sat beside Aldwych, he hung his head.

Aldwych said, "You look sad."

"I am sad, don't know why."

Aldwych thought in this case it wasn't inappropriate to put August's head on his shoulder and pat his face.

They talked for two hours. August was sad because he wasn't getting all the big roles in the new Balanchine festival, revivals of *Variations pour une Porte et un Soupir* and something else. And then he was afraid that when they went on tour he wouldn't be able to sleep without his Aldwych. They held hands; August was still naked though when he ran off to pee he did put on underpants and a T-shirt.

"And I can't bear to be away from my angel," Aldwych said, knowing how ugly he was with hair growing out of his ears and nose, as if the plan was to choke off his hearing and smell (his eyes were clouding over on their own). As he stroked the boy's bare leg he thought his sense of touch was as vivid as ever. "If only we had our own company, you could star in everything and choose the repertory and you'd never have to tour."

"What a good idea!" August exclaimed.

As they discussed it, smiling as if the idea were fantastical, August brought up several objections. He asked if Aldwych was rich enough. Aldwych said he'd have to put together a well-heeled board of Rockefellers, Phippses, Astors, and some Jews.

"Why Jews?"

Aldwych just smiled and said, "Leave that part to me."

"Are you Jewish?"

"Heavens, no. Not that I have any prejudices."

Then August said that they might not be able to get the rights to the Balanchine ballets; the estate did lease out the rights, but not to a company that might compete at home with the New York City Ballet. He said that Balanchine had left the rights to several old dancers and ex-wives, not to the company. "We'd have to commission new ballets, and that's so expensive. The new sets. The composer's fee. The choreographer's fee. The costumes. The insurance. Copies of the score for the orchestra. Everyone's salary. The hall: Where would we put our ballet? Not in the old Shriners'—the sightlines are terrible. You can't see the dancers' feet from the first ten rows. And the stage is tiny. We could revive old crowd-pleasers like *Le Corsaire*, but the staging is still expensive. To attract audiences we'd have to hire stars from other companies. The Joffrey could never make it in the long run."

All these objections were discouraging, but they were offset by the words "we" and "our." For Aldwych, nothing could be more romantic than the idea of an engrossing, life-changing project with August, one that would link their names like Nijinsky's and Diaghilev's, a relationship that seemed more mythical than sexual, or like Balanchine's and Suzanne Farrell's, creative and not at all sexual (she was a good Catholic girl, married to another dancer). An artistic legacy was what's important, not a piece of ass.

When Ernestine got wind of the ballet company she had new worries about the inheritance. Worse, Aldwych might dun her for money.

Aldwych asked August who would be a good chorographer, someone who would seem fresh, even revolutionary, but use classic ballet steps. August said, "The most original one is Dietrich of the Biarritz Ballet. I've only seen his work on YouTube, but it's great—so new and sexy. He's the greatest genius working today. And whoever does the costumes is also great." Aldwych and August settled in on the bed and watched several of Dietrich's ballets on television. Aldwych was very impressed and he loved hearing August's comments: "Their upper bodies are so strong and so are their butts. They must lift weights and do squats. And look how this redheaded kid climbs up the pole. You never see that in classical ballet. Or how they all duck under those poles. The costumes are like the circulatory system. Like those eighteenth-century anatomical machines in Naples with the beeswax arteries. So original!"

August insisted they look at the film of *Lucifer* three times. He thought it would be a good role for himself, except there were few moments to catch his breath. He loved the costumes, which were flesh-colored save for two: emerald green and acid green. He liked the way it put more emphasis on the men than on the women— homosocial, not homosexual. He didn't like the way he choreographed the ornaments and quavers ("Balanchine only sets the deep structure—but he was trained as a composer, like his brother"); he thought so many of the steps were true inventions. He also liked how all the dancers in *Lucifer* were smiling, not a ballerina's triumphant Teflon smile but playful, sensual smiles, pleasure smiles, bed smiles. And there was a solid new score.

Aldwych loved the proximity of the boy, his enthusiasm, the way his T-shirt rode up to reveal his sublime muscular waist, the way the bare skin of his biceps felt when he touched it, the muscles, though not large, tightly fit into their hairless casing, strong enough to lift Zaza to his shoulder. When he stretched and shuddered, the sudden relaxation of his entire body, the delicate boy smell that rose from his crotch excited Aldwych. They even fell asleep together for a moment and awakened in the darkness; August panicked until he realized it was his day off. He and Aldwych went to the ballet to see Zaza debut in the revival of *Ivesiana*. She was passed around the waist of the giant tree the men formed, then she stood on their shoulders, spotlit like an idol. They sat in Aldwych's usual row; luckily his usual neighbor wasn't there with her companion, and Aldwych didn't have to introduce his "nephew" to their knowing, prying smiles. They took Zaza out to dinner afterward; she was irritable about having been "mauled" by so many men during the performance, one of whom got in a few intimate feels.

Aldwych was always happy to be with Zaza. She was so sweet and pretty and ardent and uncomplicated. Maybe her sex life led her into complication, but Aldwych was simply her white dad, the man who bought her dinner and gave her little gifts and admired her and occasionally conspired with her to tighten the bonds around August. He loved being seen with her; he liked that she wasn't in her first youth. Her fondness for Aldwych wasn't naïve but was sincere, he felt. She knew every inch of August's amazing body; on tour they had shared a dressing room, even a bed, given August's fears of sleeping alone. His hands had circled her waist when she was turning, had held her trembling hand when she was about to go it alone *en pointe*, had lifted her to his shoulder. If he wasn't her man offstage, at least for thousands of fans he was her taller, stronger, enabling partner onstage, the person who stretched and supported her and bowed from the waist when she dipped a deep curtsy and as she did so, raised a surprised hand to her bony chest, her head thrown back to look gauzily at the highest balcony.

She was thrilled to hear about the ballet company and worried over the name. "Ballet West?" she wondered. "West on East? The Dupond Ballet? *Les Étoiles du Marquis Ouest?* The New Ballet?" She ordered a hearty dinner of soft-shell crabs. August was disturbed by seeing the little red legs disappear into her chewing mouth, but he coveted the boiled potatoes shaped like large olives and covered with parsley flakes and melted butter. Finally he ordered some boiled potatoes of his own; he'd seldom been that reckless before.

. . .

August's mother came for a short visit from Canada. She'd never been to the States before and knew no more than five words in English, including "Pliss" and "Sankyou." She was a neat little woman in a gray cardigan and black dress with a gilt brooch at the neck and run-down heels on her scuffed black shoes. When she smiled she revealed she was missing three teeth. She embraced August (whom she called "Eddie") and pressed him close to her, then held him at arm's length before pulling him in for another long embrace. Aldwych noticed she had tears in her eyes. When she started talking in their dialect, August begged her to speak real French for Aldwych's sake. She said very slowly in French, "I do not speak English." August laughed and said, "But we are speaking French, silly!" She looked bewildered and said *"Pas d'anglais"* and made a negating tick-tock motion with her finger. August kissed her finger and pushed her down the hall to his rooms; while she was staying with them, August had moved in with Aldwych. Soon Aldwych heard them "chirping," which he remembered was *gazouiller* in French. They had an early supper at home, a plain beef stew with a green salad, a baguette, a glass of Côtes du Rhône, and a fresh fruit macédoine; it was just

Aldwych and Marthe. August had already rushed off. He was dancing tonight.

Aldwych and Marthe scarcely understood each other but managed to have a slight conversation. The most interesting thing Aldwych learned was that August had indeed been instructed from an early age by Mme Niko-laievich in their village of Grain de Sable, a fact that August had dismissed as a lie. The lady was indeed an old Ballets Russes dancer, probably in the corps de ballet, but she had taught August all the fundamentals and praised his early promise.

Aldwych wondered why August had made up that story about pole dancing in a Montreal dive. Maybe he thought it made him seem more extraordinary, a completely self-created dancer. How weird to make up a true story, then confess it was all a lie, then learn from his mother that the "truth" about pole dancing was the real lie and the original story about ballet class was the actual truth. Or maybe he thought it was sexier to be a teenage runaway fucking tourists than to be a sweet little provincial learning to take the fifth position in a snow-bound studio run by an old chorus girl, the samovar steaming in the corner. Maybe both stories were true, that he'd studied ballet and then became a pole dancer where he was "discovered" by that New Yorker. Should he bring it up to August, or "Eddie"? He thought better of it. If the boy had reinvented himself, he must have had his reasons. When he was famous, he'd be a tough interview.

He didn't like being quizzed and didn't answer prying questions. Maybe he couldn't remember all his lies. Or maybe he lived in a constant fantasy, sometimes better than the truth, sometimes worse. That way he could be envied and pitied on alternate days. Though they were frustrating, August's ambiguities were sexy. The beloved is always mysterious.

Aldwych's seat partner and her lover were in attendance tonight, but when they heard Aldwych speaking to Marthe in French, they smiled unseeingly at some point in the middle distance and turned to each other after a crisp nod of acknowledgment. August's ballet tonight was *Rubies* to a strange, angular score by Stravinsky (he hoped she wouldn't hate it). The corps had much to do before August and Zaza came out (indeed, Marthe had thought that maybe August had been canceled for tonight's performance). Then the soloists came out in red velvet waistcoats, and August was wearing revealing white tights. His mother looked around to see if all these other adults were shocked to see so much of her son's anatomy, but they were all looking with placid, sometimes bored expressions, as if nothing could be more natural than this obscenity. She wished she could cross herself without drawing attention.

Then the lady risked her balance by falling back into Eddie's arms, but luckily he caught her. They were constantly twirling together and then apart, prancing like show horses, smiling, smiling, smiling. Then Eddie pried her legs open like a lobster's claws and Marthe braced herself for a loud cracking sound, but the lady recovered from this gynecological assault (she hoped her son would apologize to her later). They stalked around each other like stags about to fight, but then the music slowed and he slithered his arms between hers like one of those Indian goddesses and she scratched his extended palm and they kissed.

It was over, their part at least, and the audience, far from reacting disapprovingly at such risqué costumes and postures, thundered its applause.

Marthe thought it must be over, but it went on for ten minutes more of battling entrances and exits and advancing and retreating chorus boys and girls, all in red, more girls than boys. She couldn't see why Eddie was a star; all the boys seemed equally good, though one was too short and squat but had nice black hair. August and Zaza came back to dance a last bit and they got to take a solo bow onstage and then Zaza pulled out the frowsy, chubby conductor in a wilted tuxedo for his bow and he applauded the orchestra, though all but one or two musicians had left the pit already. The starring couple got two more solo bows in front of the curtain and then were joined by another lady who'd danced a comic role.

Aldwych leaned in to hear Marthe's remarks: "My son has a fine ass" (*Mon fils a un beau cul*) and "Pity he was so indecent." She said that she had seen ballet on television and she'd expected it to be more lovely, more like a fairy tale. "This one is modern," Aldwych said, as if that explained everything.

In the intermission he bought her champagne in a plastic flute.

The last ballet was a revival of *Western Symphony*. Marthe was disappointed by the cowboys (*"des rustiques"*). She was eager to get back to her son. The lesbian couple had already left during the intermission.

At dinner at Boulud's the waiter proudly brought out bottles of chilled Gatorade in a silver ice bucket. Marthe told her son that he and Zaza had danced brilliantly and she was so proud of both of them. Perhaps, August thought, my mother imagines Zaza and I are a couple. After a few more *coupes* of champagne, Marthe stood up in the aisle and demonstrated a rocking step that August and Zaza had performed. Everyone laughed. Marthe wanted to know what that step was called. No one knew. Zaza said Mr. Balanchine had invented it, she thought.

Ernestine had been seated at the end of the table with Pablo. She was telling him about her trainer from the Dominican Republic who lived in Washington Heights.

"Figures," Pablo said disdainfully. He recognized what kind of Latino she was talking about. "How much does he charge you?"

"A lot."

"And where do you work out?"

"I have a gym at home."

"Does he ever get physical with you?"

"Heavens, no. He's very professional. Why do you ask?"

"I know these guys from the D.R."

After a moment she said, "I wouldn't mind if he did."

Pablo smiled. "I thought you'd like some attention."

"Do you like women? Why are you with August?"

"My girlfriend won't take it up the ass. She doesn't like that. So I had to find a guy. That's what I like: ass. Anyway, he's the gay one—not me."

"What?"

"He's the one getting screwed, not me."

Ernestine was stunned into silence by this explanation. After her second martini on an empty stomach, her entire nervous system was filled with boiling lead. She found, to her surprise, that her hand was on Pablo's knee. After a while he moved it to his crotch, which she stroked experimentally, though it took her a moment to figure it out anatomically. It was all brawny contours. The mother kept calling August "Eddie." His ass had looked big and muscular tonight and Pablo couldn't wait to climb back into it.

Marthe stayed two more days. Ernestine offered to take her shopping, but August doubted they had the same taste, budget, or . . . language. Anyway, his mother wanted to spend as much time as possible with her "Eddie," though he had to forbid her to come to class (bringing your mother to ballet exercises!). On her last day she grew strangely cold to Aldwych; he reviewed all their interactions and couldn't put his finger on what had gone wrong. He phoned Zaza, who said, "She thinks you're a vampire drinking the blood of her beautiful son. I tried to head her off at the pass by telling her I was the one who was sleeping with August. She told me she was convinced Eddie alas was *comme ça* even though the Holy Father had condemned Athenian acts if not Athenians themselves if they were chaste. But she saw how that old man, she said, was sharing a bed with her little boy. I think it is your age, Aldwych, she is objecting to more than your sex. I reminded her that August couldn't fall asleep if alone and I said that Pablo was August's 'partner.' She found that more acceptable as long as the penis was attached to someone young. It's like straight kids—if a twenty-two-year-old seduces an eighteen-year-old girl, that's cool, but if he's thirty he's a criminal."

"You're wonderful, Zaza."

She squeezed his hand. He really did feel blessed to have such a friend.

. . .

August went with Aldwych to the dentist. They were shown into an examining room almost immediately. A big television was showing twin brothers rebuilding "unsalable" houses, turning them into modernized barns with up-to-date kitchens and large, fenced-in wooden decks. One of the identical twins had a beard but they both had the same smiles and thin legs.

A clinician came in and took X-rays of August's teeth. She didn't seem shocked by the oral ruin. When the chipper handsome gay dentist came in and was looking at the X-rays, he said, "We'll have to send you to Dr. Diamondstein in the Village—an oral surgeon—to have D6 and D7 and A3 pulled. They're so loose it won't be hard to do, and you won't feel a thing. Then we'll make you plastic temporaries and, when the gums are healed, permanents."

"I only have three more weeks in New York before I go out of town for several weeks."

"The temporaries will look good, but you'll have to eat carefully with them, since they can crack; they're plastic, after all." He promised they'd have the temporaries in by the time he left town. "Where you going?"

"Saratoga. I'm a dancer."

"I used to know Jacques d'Amboise."

The dental surgeon, Dr. Diamondstein, was painless. He was very handsome with his copious black chest hair shooting up out of the V of his blue medical smock. He told August he was engaged but was not marrying his fiancé for another year. August wondered why two men would wait that long if they were really in love; maybe their mothers wanted to have a very elaborate wedding with a hundred people for a seated dinner under tents in their Westchester backyard and pictures of the boys in the *Times* on the society page, and all that took planning.

Back at the regular dentist August had to bite down into molds filled with blue chemical mud. A week later his temporaries were ready and glued in place. He took a selfie grimacing to show his upper and lower teeth for his mother; he looked like a gargoyle. Within a day he smiled more easily than he ever had, was less shy, less suspicious.

Aldwych thought he needed a better reason for starting a new ballet company than just showcasing his boyfriend. He got Thierry Dietrich's email address and wrote him in his imperfect French (his speaking was more convincing than his writing) to suggest that he might like a New York season and that he, Aldwych, could fly to Biarritz for a "conversation." The choreographer responded positively two days later and Aldwych immediately booked a round-trip fare to Paris and tickets on the high-speed train to Biarritz, where he reserved a suite overlooking the sea in the ugly hotel built by Napoleon III for his Spanish wife, Eugénie.

He felt pathologically lonely for August. He checked the time and it was the wrong hour to call the boy. He knew it was tactically wise to be not so smothering, to be at least occasionally unavailable. Not that it was such a clever ruse—people did go on trips, they did fall asleep, they weren't yearning 24/7. If he played his most daring card, August wouldn't even notice; Aldwych would finally seem like a normal human being: independent, busy, preoccupied, multitasking. But his only task was to make himself indispensable to August, to close the millimeter separating them.

He walked along the wide white sand beach. It was deserted, though there was one man way out on the cement pier. He was wearing a chic pale blue raincoat. Fifty years ago Aldwych had bought one like that in Rome on the Via dei Condotti; the salesman had had the cheek to say "And it is even rain resistant," as if that was an unusual feature in a raincoat. There was too much park furniture on the beach; Europeans rarely understood the beauty of what they called "wild beaches."

He'd been in love like this six times in his life, only the first time with a girl in high school. Was Aldwych someone destined always to be unhappy in love? What he felt wasn't a sweet absence but a cataclysmic panic. Would his last desire be to receive a kiss from the executioner, to fuse with the driver of the other car hurtling toward his? Why did he feel so perilously alone? As though he were drowning in the undertow and unable to find the ground under the roiling waves? He knew he had come into this world alone, a red, gasping, slimy homunculus, his head squeezed between unyielding walls of bleeding flesh, the cord wrapped perilously tight around his neck. And that he would leave it gasping again, stanched with vomit, clutching his burning heart, alone, looking around wildly for a helping hand, someone to accompany him. There would be no hand.

Each solitude felt unique, as if he were dying because Stan, or Troy, or Giuseppe, or Keith, or Jim Ruddy, or

August was irreplaceable, the one man predetermined to save or savage him. The pain was always the same; only the faces changed, indelible when they were in the frame, not yet divined when still unspooled, forgotten when relayed to the gathering reel.

It occurred to him to look up a great past love on Facebook to see if he was still alive and if so how time had worked over the woodcut of his face with its burin. If he'd known the tides would have eaten the beloved's face down to the bones, would he ever have been so violently in love? The blond hair curling on the strong, tanned neck, the eyes gray and white like coldwater agates, the fine dusting of gold powder on the cheeks, the lips an improbable red, the skin that would be pink if it hadn't been khakied by the sun . . . To think that all that had faded, that that slithering mail had turned into harsh bars of lead, that the subtle colors had been drained, that the delicate hand-carved features had been thickened and copied in lard. It was hard to love someone ugly unless he or she had been ugly and lovable since the beginning: "a character."

. . .

The Biarritz Ballet Company was housed in an old railroad station that had been restored and reconstructed into a large theater, practice rooms, and offices. The building, of light-colored stone, had two square towers: *The French*, Aldwych thought, *know how to do this sort of thing*. He was accompanied to Dietrich's office by a striking tall skinny boy with violet eyes, nearly purple lips, and a promisingly large Adam's apple. Whereas the boy seemed terminally shy, Dietrich himself was bristling with energy—balding, muscular, chiseled, with big lustrous eyes. When he spoke he overarticulated in a gay way, as if in society he needed to assert himself unnaturally in order for his aggressiveness to serve his quirky, inner-looking creativity, to be the hard shell around the soft center.

He was sitting on a tufted couch that seemed somehow stranded in the midst of the sleek, nearly empty office, as if it were a period piece forgotten backstage when the stage-hands had struck the set. He stood and gave Aldwych a hot, wet hand. *Oh, good*, Aldwych thought, *he's nervous too.*

When he heard Aldwych stumble in French, he switched to English but Aldwych, unbowed, continued in French and eventually won the day.

"I've had my dances in Texas and some other states but never in New York," he said matter-of-factly. "I guess I'm not aggressive enough. In Dallas we danced without sets, which arrived only a day late." He paused and smiled for the first time. "I asked around and found out you are very rich and undoubtedly know other rich people. That's all *comme il faut*, but I don't understand your interest in ballet."

Aldwych looked at the floor and then stared directly into Dietrich's eyes. "Can I tell you the truth?"

"As you wish." Pause. "I can't imagine you were ever a dancer."

"No, never." He took a deep breath. "My lover is a dancer. A famous dancer."

"A happy kept boy (*un gigolo heureux*)?"

"Not at all. He really loves me."

"And does he make love to you, or is it an intellectual companionship?"

"It's both! He likes to fuck me at least three times a day. He'll even come home *en vitesse* if he has a free half hour to get another fuck in."

"You lucky man. You are *comblé*—fulfilled!"

"And we talk to each other for hours—about art, life, love."

"I've always wanted a lover like that," the choreographer said wistfully.

"But what about all these boys around you?"

He looked annoyed. "Now, what was it exactly you wanted to talk about?"

"My friend, who is an *étoile* of the New York City Ballet—his name is August Dupond—he and I would like to start a new New York ballet company and use your choreography."

"Why?"

"Because you're the world's greatest—"

"Perhaps, but why another ballet company in New York?"

"The New York ballet audience is growing stronger every year. At least that's my impression."

"To the point of supporting a new company for an entire season?"

"Couldn't we share you with Biarritz?"

"Why would I want to do that? Or the town fathers of Biarritz, for that matter?"

"Frankly, you're not that famous in the States. Few people know your name."

"Only the people who count."

"In Dallas, perhaps. In France they know you in Pau, St. Etienne, even in Réunion."

Dietrich lifted a warning finger and Aldwych muttered, *"Je m'excuse."*

"Unlike some people I have little admiration for America. I'll admit Balanchine was a genius, but he was Russian, like that other American genius, Strawinski. I don't give a damn if I'm unknown in America." He pronounced it in a swallowed, abbreviated form emphasizing *amer*—"bitter".

"After two or three reviews in New York you'll be famous there, too."

"Fame is very *inconstante*. But do you think I'll make your August the star of my company? He hasn't learned our style of dancing."

"He's watched *Lucifer* thirty times and has even performed the first half of it for me. Wait till you see him. He's as good as Nureyev or Baryshnikov."

"Why not throw Erik Bruhn into the pot as well? Or do you only like Americanized Russians? Is your August Russian?"

"No. French. French Canadian."

"I'm basing a new ballet, which I'm rehearsing in an hour, on Lévi-Strauss and Samuel Beckett."

"That sounds very French."

"Thank you. You may sit in if you like. Remember, we have twenty dancers, a small orchestra, wardrobe and makeup artists, tons of scenery, lights, lighting designers . . ."

"It sounds as if we have a deal."

"Why would your August give up the New York City Ballet for the Dietrich?"

"You must ask him."

"That's not good enough."

"Don't underestimate the power of your choreography."

"I don't."

"The only thing I don't like is when you choreograph the ornaments with little twittering fingers. Balanchine doesn't do that—only the deep structure."

"You must have read that somewhere. That's not something a non-dancer would notice." It was true. He'd heard it from August.

. . .

That night in the hotel he subscribed again to his favorite porn site (but only for one month, nonrecurring) and looked at a dumb bleached blond with an enormous cock attack a slender but wizened boy half his size who spoke with a dirty mouth that didn't go with his preppy looks. The boy said his favorite activity was having his butt kissed from the coccyx down and then rimmed. The boy kept his jock strap on; perhaps his cock was embarrassingly small.

The dumb blond obliged him and ate out his hole for twenty minutes while the boy kept moaning and saying, "Fuck!" Every once in a while the blond came up for air and said "Fuck!" in a much deeper voice. The boy began to suck the enormous cut dick. He said in a prissy but sincere voice, "This is the biggest cock I've ever seen. Or sucked." The blond seemed unfazed by the compliment. His eyes were half closed and he said the kid's mouth felt really good. After a while the kid straddled the blond's mouth, then the top went back to rimming him while the kid sucked the big dick (even opening wide he could only get it halfway down). Then the blond man laid him on his back and held the kid's legs open, dived down to his hole for another few licks, then asked in an uninterrogatory voice, "You want this big dick in you?" The boy whispered a hissed assent. The blond placed his wide penis head into the anus and filled it completely, then pulled it out playfully. The boy began to moan almost autonomically. He looked at the glans; the squamous cells were simple squares, the kind a child might draw on the sidewalk, but smaller. The whole thick, rigid thing looked like a battering ram, nerveless and invincible but attentive and on the hunt, searching for a dirty hole to invade. Maybe it was smelling the air for ass. It could have been a very primitive animal with keen olfactory bulbs and a shape designed to push into a ripe, waiting wetness.

Aldwych was both participant and spectator, performer and witness. He scrutinized their perfection with the soul's spyglass and felt the penis abusing his glottis, then his rectum. He pushed a finger into himself like an old-fashioned gas tank gauge. His hand, he reasoned, was as good as another man's, but it didn't feel as good. He tweaked his own nipples and gasped, "Oh, August."

The blond suddenly pulled down the kid's jock strap and the kid had a decent dick after all, bigger than normal, skinned clean and narrow but long and erect; the blond set to work sucking it methodically and the twink said, a bit nasally, "Yes, excellent! Suck that cock." The real problem with the twink was his haircut, arranged and parted perfectly, held in place by a plasticizing spray.

The hung blond went back to fucking the twink; they were facing each other and kissing. The kid's legs were pressed open like a wishbone and one wondered if they'd break apart and who would get the winning bigger half. The boy kept saying the blond was so "big" and so "deep."

Then he said accusingly, "You're going to make me cum," and the blond dug deeper and faster. The kid spilled cloudy thick cum all over his hairless tummy; then the blond pulled out, lay beside the boy, applied himself, and ejaculated. The kid was still fist-pumping though he'd already shot. They pulled apart, smiled as if they were only now awakening, and kissed coolly, matrimonially.

Aldwych looked down at the meager spritz he'd ejaculated on his hairy, flabby stomach with its unappetizing
bottom fold of flesh. He couldn't usually cum and had
mostly given up trying but he'd been so excited by
watching the new Heidegger ballet that afternoon that
he'd turned back to his favorite porn site. All those
gasping, sweating French and Spanish men with their big
muscled rumps and legs as powerful as oak trunks, their
sweat-stained practice clothes and their long Romantic
hair, the girls' heavenly thin waists passing through the
eye of a partner's cupped hands, the darting exit of a ballerina whose pointe shoe ribbons had come undone and
her quick return after she'd set herself to rights, the strong
stresses and missed notes of the out-of-tune upright piano,
the sudden thump of the men landing in unison on the
springy studio floor—all that adrenaline had excited him,
and the porn stars had put him over the top.

As he returned into the earth's gravitational pull and
looked around at the heavy damask curtains and the
many wall mirrors, he was filled with a devastating
postcoital vacancy, the disappointment you experience
when you finally arrive in Thebes and discover it's a
ghost town. And he felt the tiniest trace of resentment
at having shared his space capsule with handsome
cosmonauts and now having landed in an icy sea of soli-
tary self-hatred. When he was with beauties like August
he could be attractive by association, but he wasn't
ready for reality when he stumbled into the mirrored

bathroom in search of a washcloth to clean up his all-too-manageable mess.

He phoned August on his cell. It was only six in the evening there. "I have good news. Dietrich is very excited about our proposal."

"Oh, great. When is he coming over?"

"Next February, if I can get the rental and money and visas all worked out."

"That's great! Is he nice?"

"As the English would say, *quite*. No, seriously, he's very shrewd and serious as he should be. It's his company and his repertory, after all."

"I wonder if he'll like me."

"He's very eager to work with you. I showed him the video of you in *Agon*—he was very impressed," Aldwych lied.

After all these years, Aldwych hadn't learned to dose out his affirmations; too wide a currency lowered their value. Aldwych's wholehearted compliments would have been stronger if they had been halfhearted.

When he looked full-on at his memory of the pornography, he resented it for excluding him; if he glimpsed it through his peripheral vision, he treasured the inclusion. He replayed the positions and mumbled words in his mind as he looked out at the clouds on the plane ride home. Hugely satisfying as that film clip had been, he didn't want to watch it again yet; he'd prefer to discover the unseen ones. He watched an American action movie on the plane and a French one about love. The action film made him forget himself; the romantic film made him reflect on his own life with bittersweetness. He'd known landscaped domains like the one in France but had rarely met such beautiful *figurants*. His theory, nevertheless, was that most small and avid pig-faced millionaires had tall blond beautiful children because they could afford lovely wives; look at Barron Trump. For the rest of his trip he was happy because the porn stars had been unwitting accomplices to a rare sex act of his own. Like summer lightning on a sunny day, however, anxious thoughts about the expenses and exhaustion of the pending ballet project broke into his general contentment. But he was sure he was being brave and might yet win August's love.

He arrived in the early afternoon and looked idly around to see if August might have come to meet his plane. Of course he wasn't there; they'd agreed it was a foolish waste of time to make airport trips; no one did that except the cousins of Bulgarian refugees.

It was a mid-June day, bright and sunny, and he liked both the speed and the predictable slowness of the taxi darting down the FDR—slowness because he'd made this trip a thousand, two thousand times in his long life and knew all the landmarks. Of course August was off in class, limbering up; he was dancing *Prodigal Son* tonight, only his third time. The maid and the cook were both there to greet him, as was a heart-covered note from August: *Soit le Bienvenu!* Canadians in their picturesque way even used an anglicism, "Bienvenu," in response to "Merci" though the French themselves said nothing or, deprecatingly, *"Je vous en prie."*

That afternoon after class August returned with a pretty, effeminate boy, young and short and too sure of himself, who stuck his hand out and said, "I'm Arnold. Are you the mysterious roommate?"

"I guess I am," Aldwych said sourly. He noticed the boy was wearing eyeliner.

August looked embarrassed and said, "I thought you were coming back tomorrow."

Aldwych shrugged but remembered to smile and retreated to his room, tears in his eyes.

He wept and wept with waves of what he called "self-pity," as if anything less reprehensible wouldn't prompt so much emotion. He bit the back of his hand so he wouldn't sob out loud. He felt ignoble and jealous and surprised that August had forgotten his return date and that August, who rarely brought anyone to bed, had chosen someone so unappealing, such a weird combination of brazen and feminine. Was August a closet top? Thinking August had *un goût exclusif* for oversexed ruffians like Pablo had somehow consoled Aldwych, who couldn't see his way to fulfilling that role. But at this very moment he must be lubricating the ass of that boy, who was undoubtedly complaining about the delay and August's distracted lack of ardor. That was an imperious little ass, Aldwych could see, quick to take offense or sense rejection, quick to gobble down any offering.

Maybe something like a fiasco did take place, because a minute later and half an hour sooner than expected, Arnold was slamming the front door in anger. August knocked lightly on Aldwych's door and came in before Aldwych said anything.

August looked surprised and lifted a hand but withdrew it. "You've been crying? Why? Because I brought that silly Arnold home? Because I forgot when you were flying home?"

The word "home" sounded tonelessly through Aldwych and made him start crying again. He turned his head to disguise his anguish from his "roommate." "I thought you'd welcome me home," he said with a wavering smile and a broken voice and a look of gleaming shame in his eyes.

Something about the situation clearly made August furious. Maybe he hated being obliged to feel guilty. Or maybe he hated Aldwych's concession to suffering—Aldwych was sure the runaway boy with the pious, narrow-minded parents must have learned to brave his way stoically out to personal freedom. He probably couldn't bear to see an intimate friend give way to flagrant pain. August's face was frozen with contempt. "Look," he said, "I hope you're not going to play the wounded lover. I told you from the very beginning that we weren't lovers and would never be lovers. That was made crystal clear before I moved in." The way he accented the c in *crystal* and *clear* frightened Aldwych. August would make no concessions, obviously, and Aldwych's unspoken appeal for clemency only irritated him all the more.

Aldwych said, "What happened with your friend?"

"He disgusts me. So do you."

"Me? What have I done? I've been battling for our ballet company."

"Rich people don't battle. They have whims, caprices." August said *caprice* in the French way. "Anyway, I'm not sure I want to leave the New York City Ballet. I've struggled for years"—and for August it did feel like years—"to get where I am. Besides, they're going to give me the lead in the new Justin Peck. Apparently he likes me, Peck."

"Who wouldn't?

"He's married."

Aldwych was disgusted by the vulgarity of that remark. He didn't like unforgiving, rigid categories like "straight" and "gay."

And August's dangerous fickleness.

August kissed Aldwych, shook his head slowly, and said, "What am I going to do with you?"

Aldwych looked up through still watery eyes and smiled slightly, mainly from embarrassment.

August said, "I'll join you soon and finally get a good night's sleep."

"And who was that . . . tart, if I may ask?"

"Just a kid who hangs out at the stage door, wears too much perfume, and worships dancers to the point of resenting them." After a second they both broke into a laugh as the boy's remark registered. The hatchet had been buried, but only slightly.

. . .

That night, before his performance, as he was putting on his makeup and costume and gelling his hair, August asked himself again whether the rich can ever like or even understand the poor. He could still remember when he broke free of the ex-dancer who'd "discovered" him and brought him to New York, who'd become colder and ruder, really insufferable, as August had become a better and better dancer and at seventeen been offered a scholarship at the School of the New York City Ballet. Edgar (that was his name!) wasn't rich but he'd saved his money (including his fee for that one dance movie) and invested it and even now he never bought new clothes or fresh flowers and he could stretch out a pot roast for three dinners and a lunch.

August had left in a fury after a trick of Edgar's had left his bed and knocked on August's door. The boy had said no, but Edgar had worked himself into a rage of jealousy and had told August he must move out, he needed to rent out the room, for which he could get the thousand a month he badly needed.

August didn't say anything but packed all his belongings and left, saying he'd pick up his bag the next day and would leave his key on the dinner table. It was nine on a cool October night, but the boy couldn't bear to stay another moment at Edgar's. He had seven dollars in his wallet and he headed uptown to Fifty-Third and Third, which he knew was a hustler's pickup place in front of the post office. He hadn't eaten since the Rice Krispies he'd had in the morning before class. His first john wanted him to waltz nude around his small, cluttered apartment while he, the customer, beat off. The music was some horrible Johann Strauss. The guy, tubby and in his forties with hair on his back, was naked except for piss-stained drawers he'd pulled down to his thighs. He kept muttering things to excite himself that August couldn't hear because the music was so loud. After it was over he seemed put out that August wanted to take a quick shower. He handed over the four twenties reluctantly and resentfully and even said, "I've only paid once before. I never have trouble getting freebies but tonight I wanted a Waltz King scenario. I've always wanted to make films." He sighed. "I'd never hire you again. Too skinny. And I'm not turned on by uncut dick. But you dance all right. By the way, you have an accent—where are you from?"

"Montenegro." It was fun making up fake facts; the only problem was you had to remember them. He liked inventing things; that way these guys didn't possess you in any way.

"I thought so. Montenegro? What are they known for?"

"Vendettas."

From talking to another student he found he could share a room with him ("no funny business," the guy assured him) in Long Island City. "After class we can go out and see it. It's just five hundred a month. No security up front. It's a nice quiet house. Orthodox Jewish couple." August hastily agreed. The kid laughed. "You might have to switch a lamp on for them on Saturdays. Sabbath goy." He explained they were forbidden to do anything on Saturdays, their Sabbath. "They cook everything in advance. They can't push an elevator button. Nothing." August nodded enthusiastically. "Is it okay if a goy cooks?"

"Sure. They don't care."

The guy, Marty, said he could wait another week for the rent. He was a very nice guy from Florida. Orlando. His stepmom had danced on Disney cruises until, as she put it, she'd "hooked" Marty's father, a passenger and a recent divorcé. She was a very positive force and got Marty into dance class right away.

That afternoon he retrieved his suitcase and left his house key. He could hear Edgar rattling around in his room but August didn't call out to him.

His john that night had a pencil-thin mustache, lived in a high-rise in Murray Hill, owned a full set of weights in the bedroom, and displayed an unhealthy interest in August's rectum. He prepared an entire dinner for August and watched him eat every bite. He explained he wanted to take part in a "blumpkin"—that Eddie (the name August was using) would sit on the toilet and shit while the john knelt between his legs and performed fellatio.

On Fifty-Third Street they'd agreed on $100, but for normal gay sex. "This blumpkin is a bit unusual," August said. "I'll need three hundred for that."

The john quickly agreed and paid up, his hands shaking with desire.

August hated gays, but he hated being gay himself even more.

10

Pablo's card said that he was a "masseuse"; Ernestine wondered if there were some hidden, dismaying meaning in the use of the feminine. She messaged him asking if he did two-hour sessions and would he do one tomorrow at noon in her room at the Pierre, then they'd have room service lunch at two unless he was otherwise engaged. Ernestine reminded him of her last name and told him the Pierre was at 2 East Sixty-First. She didn't want to sound condescending, but you never knew with these people. Better vexed than clueless.

Ernestine bathed, did a touch-up depilation, and even gave herself a cleansing enema (just in case—it was not her favorite kind of sex but it was his, apparently). She dressed herself very simply with lewd underwear; Pablo was probably magnetized by the most extreme sluttishness. (She chose heart-shaped nipple cutouts, contour speedlines edged in red-lip lace cupping the squeezed-up breasts, features of an otherwise flesh-colored strappy push-up balcony bra.) She put on a black lace thong, the provocative underclothes belied by a simple pastel blue cotton poplin shirt dress, collar tipped up *à la lesbienne*, and her great-aunt's negligée necklace with a white opal rose gold pendant. She wondered if Pablo would be intimidated by the front desk staff standing about stiffly in cutaways, but he arrived, knocked audibly if feebly on her door, and walked in wearing a cologne that smelled like bubble gum and jeans he must be wearing commando style since there was a large bulge to the right of the fly buttons. He kissed the edge of her mouth glancingly, went directly to the window, pulled back the vaporous curtains, and stared down on Central Park.

"Want a whiskey from the mini-bar?"

"I don't like whiskey—too fattening. Got any tequila? Less sugar."

She thought this a curiously vain preference for a real man but rooted around in the fridge knowing how attractive her ass must look from this angle (she had a talent for seeing herself from every perspective). She found a lone split of Cuervo Gold and helplessly handed it to him with a glass. He bobbed his head in thanks. Pointing to the bed, he asked, "Is this where we're going to work? I should have brought my table. Bad angle for my back. Well, you should strip down. They must have a terry cloth robe in your size if you're shy."

She didn't want him to miss out on her lingerie so she unbuttoned her overstarched shirt dress; the button-holes resisted her fingers but eventually she stood before him in Victoria's Open Secret. He whistled and said "Not bad for a mature woman," which she reasoned herself into taking as a compliment. "I usually work in the nude," he added. In a moment he had stepped out of his sockless loafers and his jeans (yep, no underwear) and pulled off his T-shirt advertising a rock band she'd never heard of. He had tiny nipples, nearly black, hair-less, that would tempt no one to suck them. Under his taut chest was surprising military brass—obliques and lats, a stripe for every year of working out, a solid wall of strength.

After her third orgasm (two digital, one genital) they ate their crustless *pain de mie* chicken salad sandwiches, extra mayonnaise. She had put the three-hundred-dollar fee in an unsealed Pierre envelope. All Pablo could talk about was his growing reputation as a "masseuse." He claimed he had a soap opera TV actress among his clients as well as a music executive, who liked his butt played with but who was really straight.

. . .

At the same hour on the same day Aldwych was meeting with his lawyer, Laurence Butterfield, in the white Wall Street Building with its shiny brass fixtures and its black doors incised with intaglio patterns, its imposing bulk crowding every inch of its footprint like a man who's grown too fat for his slippers. Laurence always looked as if he was about to step out the window into his yacht; he'd known a girl who'd dated him and said he had no odor, no smell whatsoever. Once Laurence told him that he'd felt such an oddball at St. Paul's; Aldwych's then wife had said, "Laurence, if *you*, whose ancestor was a judge in Puritan Boston and started Harvard or something—if *you* felt like an outsider, then there's no hope for any of us." They'd all laughed.

True to form, Laurence was wearing an ascot, a blazer, creepily thin white ankle socks and Top-Siders, pressed khakis as though he'd dropped in only for a moment. He was exuding a very strong scent Aldwych recognized from his Paris days—Aventus by Creed. On the wood-paneled walls were hung five nineteenth-century prints of American clippers with their narrow hulls and expansive sails. Laurence shook hands in a great wave of cologne and moved from his desk to a gray love seat. Smiling, he patted the space beside him. The person who'd accompanied Aldwych down the hall stopped back in to take coffee orders.

In his preppy version of "Whassup?" Laurence asked, "To what do I owe the pleasure . . . ?"

Aldwych said, "I want to start my own ballet company."

"Good lord! If you'd said you wanted to write a blank verse tragedy about a fourteenth-century pedophile I couldn't have been more astonished." He waited for the remark to land. "Well, you're rich, but is anyone rich enough to do *that?*"

"Maybe I can put together a board of rich layabouts."

"So what inspired you? A sexy little raven-haired coryphée?"

"It's a boy, actually." He looked up at a clipper print. "You must have guessed I was always walking on the wild side."

"He must be quite the looker. Personally, I could never get over the barrier of fucking a hairy asshole. Even at St. Paul's—remember Dickie Enfield? I was sort of in love with him, *faute de mieux*, but the one time I actually examined his asshole my erection melted."

"I don't have those scruples." Aldwych didn't dare admit he'd only touched August that one spit-roasting time. And that hustler time he couldn't remember.

"Far be it from me to impose my aesthetics on anyone else. Who is he?"

"French Canadian. A star in the New York City Ballet. He already lives with me. His name is August. He's twenty."

"Sounds like he'll ruin even a very rich man like you."

"He can do whatever he wishes to me."

Laurence bowed his head in resignation or perhaps respect for *l'amour fou*. They spent the next half hour reviewing Aldwych's finances. As Aldwych was leaving, Laurence said, "If you get too crazy, Ernestine and I can always impose a conservatorship on you."

. . .

At exactly noon the same day, August and Zaza sat down at the nearly deserted Café Luxembourg (Aldwych had recommended it for her birthday); by the time they left ninety minutes later, it had filled up. August had called up the day before for two slices of carrot cake, one of them with a pink candle.

Neither of them had been there before, but they admired, without commenting on, the red leather booths, the big windows and mirrors, the vertical yellow tubular wall lights set in chrome fixtures, the wooden bar, the chic servers, the salmon starters and the branzino main, the Parisian small portions, the constant, silent circulating of the busboys, the bright striped Covid sidewalk café, the shouting American customers who were making so much noise by the end of their meal that they didn't notice they'd run out of things to say. That was the best thing about Americans: they took up all the oxygen and you never had to search for conversation.

Zaza was so touched that August had invited her to this expensive, festive restaurant where all the male waiters were suspiciously good-looking. She wondered who the queer headwaiter must be.

For a while they talked about the morning class. Zaza said, "That was so funny when Olga (she's so tiny!) looked right at Olf and said, 'Don't look at yourself in the mirror. That is forbidden.' Olf just turned away *effacé* and I think he actually turned red, or, in his pale Swedish case, *pink*. Did you notice his very tight practice clothes, the sweatshirt that said '*Well?*'"

"Those purple tights! A doctor could have done a complete physical without his undressing at all. Did those *battements*, quick *entrechats*, *pirouettes* going into arabesque—did they exhaust you?"

"They were exhausting, but Olga is always so sweet, and I liked the way everyone applauded her specially long and she looked so embarrassed and kept saying, 'Silly! Silly! You're so silly.'"

"I like the way she calls us all, men and women, 'guys.'" I was really sweating at the end."

"Me, too! Do I smell?"

"Of course not."

"Seriously?"

"You're so pink you almost look like a white person."

"Shut up!" Joking about her "Asian looks" was an important part of their comic routine.

"And you don't look too gay today," she said.

"Shut up!" They subsided into a familiar moment of contented hostility.

August asked, "Could you go to bed with Olga?"

"And get a mouthful of silky white pubes? Eww . . ."

They drank their Diet Cokes. A fan, an overweight Asian in Yamamoto, begged August to autograph his newspaper. August complied and looked away, and the man bowed his way back to his table.

Zaza said, "I'm worried your mother thinks Aldwych is molesting you."

"How silly."

"You know how rotten my French is, but I think I told her you were just loving friends."

"Someone must have put that in her head. Wait—her favorite show for years was *La Main au Collet—To Catch a Predator?*"

"I hated that show. These poor lonely men lured into suburban hot tubs by actresses pretending to be teens and as soon as the man eased into the Jacuzzi a whole team of cameras and spray-tan presenters came rushing in to embarrass everyone."

"I never heard a woman object to that series, heartless as it was; my mother relished every humiliation, especially when the hapless predator ran out in his undies and was tackled by the cops. Then the unsmiling *présentateur* started his somber moralizing."

"Well, I think your mother wants to *catch* poor Aldwych."

"That's crazy. He's never even touched me except years ago when he hired me as a seventy-five-dollar hustler."

"What? Stop!"

"I was broke and hungry. He picked me up on Third Avenue and couldn't wait to get me out the door."

The Russian waiter came by for the third time and asked them if everything was all right. They assured him it was—*except for the hectoring service*, August thought. The waiter shrugged and smiled. At five o'clock he had a big screen test for a Visionworks commercial. He didn't have to say anything with his weird accent—just put on some eyeglasses and look astonished. No more orders from these American animals. Since the pandemic, most "guests" were irritable, he and the other "waitstaff" agreed.

Zaza said, "Is Aldwych really going to start a new ballet company for you and bring that French choreographer over? Won't you miss us?"

August squeezed her hand and they kissed like two silver Art Deco figurines, no tongue, just brushing closed lips. For some reason the waiter thought of a borzoi— were those the sleek dogs on book spines? The "sighthound?" He decided to annoy them by asking them again how the service was.

They didn't respond.

"Am I making the mistake of my life?" August asked.

"Let's think. You're at the height of your powers and you have a famous company backing you."

"Not always. They stood in my way for a long time."

"Six months."

"That's an eternity for a dancer."

She asked for a lemonade ("No sugar, I *like* it bitter"), then ran her hand through her hair. "You like that French guy—"

"Alsatian."

"But what if the critics over here don't go for him? Or even review him?"

"They have to review him. Don't they?"

"Well, it's true you'd have new choreography, new costumes, new music, new partners—"

"The same old orchestra conductor."

"But he's good!" Zaza exclaimed in protest.

"You're right. Never too fast or slow. I wanted our own ballet company at first because I was getting great reviews but no new roles. You know how short our careers are. I got super-paranoid and thought it was because I was too gay. Or just gay. But now I'm getting some great roles and Peck is making his new dance on me. But will it last? I can feel all these talented boys breathing on my heels."

"Peck's great!"

"So I feel like a brat complaining."

"And you are a star of the world's best-known company."

"I *am* a brat. But now what do I do with Aldwych? He's so into this! The sorcerer's apprentice."

"Is the service satisfactory?"

"Two coffees, please."

"What, no dessert? We have a delicious Reine Claude plum tartelette. Tempted?"

"Coffee," August said coldly. "And I ordered two slices of carrot cake for my friend's birthday."

"Iced antique brandy?"

"No!" He'd observed Aldwych when he was vexed. He didn't need everyone to like him. August thought he should grow up and take his place in the world.

II

A few months later they had their first snow (was it November already?) but Aldwych was so busy planning their ballet he scarcely noticed the hour or the day or the season. In all his long, leisurely life he'd never been so *affairé*. Till now his life had been a long dormitory bull session. He'd never cut short a conversation, for instance, because he had three more calls to make before five. He'd never sprung out of bed; in fact, he'd never set an alarm unless he had an early morning plane to catch or meet. His psychoanalyst had always been impressed by how fertile his dream life was and wondered why it had suddenly dried up. Aldwych was too embarrassed to admit that in the past he'd always slept in as long as he liked and that a lazy awakening best facilitates late morning dreams and remembering them, whereas his current diet of panicked early morning appointments and the fuss of finding and silencing an alarm clock shredded the gossamer wings of dream dragonflies. He had no inner life now, or a very shallow one. Dreams and daydreams flourish in the soft vagaries of a peaceful, retired existence, punctuated only by the rites of hygiene and the shifting regime of meals. In the past he'd had no habits, no obligations, no chores; as that French novel had declared, "As for living, our servants can do it for us." Now he had some hectic life of his very own.

In the past he'd been nice to people in a rambling, pointless, spontaneous, nearly ritualistic way—nothing to gain except human warmth, the occasional sexual adventure, amusement, prestige. Most of the people he knew he'd known forever—Princeton Day School, St. Paul's, an "extra man" at countless debutante balls, athletic team weekends ("Go, Tigers!"), in his late twenties twice a best man, often a wedding guest, weekends in Bar Harbor, Nantucket, the Hamptons, Martha's Vineyard—and in the winter Vail. They were not people you wanted to impress. You had already gained admission just by your pedigree, because you'd always been around. He liked to say that the people in his circle were like the Greek gods, vaguely related to one another, all a bit self-centered, not evil but inevitable and eternal and free to play their emblematic roles, to each an ascribed virtue or vice. The odd political or religious views of childhood friends could not be examined in detail or squabbled over; those views were an attribute, unchanging and divine. Besides, their parents had warned them never to discuss religion or politics at the table—and now they understood why. Though most Americans said they prized friendship over marriage and family, studies showed they had fewer and fewer friends (men even fewer than women). Undoubtedly the loudmouths on social media had made it all worse and reduced everyone to tribes of one.

Now that he was trying to put together a board of rich patrons, he sized up these childhood friends by a different standard; he was like a eunuch who's grown a pair and looks at women with new interest. Leonard told him off the record who in their circle were seriously rich and who wasn't ("Poor Edwin, he may have been a walker for Nancy Reagan but he's got only six million dollars"). Some of them had rich, famous relatives and were worth "cultivating" (he'd never thought of people before as valuable shrubs) though they owned only a shabby brownstone on Fifty-Third next to a Costco and she had sold hats at Lord & Taylor. That woman, some sort of cousin, was friends with the Lambert bankers from Belgium—and Laurence thought that was a promising "contact" (he'd never before heard such words).

He hired a small staff of three young people, one a law student (male) and two women who wanted careers in nonprofit arts administration. He had to ask his cook what was considered a good salary in New York and was surprised it was so high. He quickly learned that if he was in a bad mood, the employees would panic and be convinced the whole enterprise was about to go down the drain. He was always upbeat, remembered their names and the names of their mates and children. He wrote these details down in a new notebook, along with their birthdays, alma mater / major, whether they were vegan / vegetarian / lactose or glucose or fructose intolerant / allergic to peanuts / A.A. / hated oysters / shrimp-queasy / had to eat whole grains / hours of intermittent fasting / Jewish? Observing? Kosher? Americans, he knew, were very particular about these things. Some hostesses printed up a checklist before inviting guests to dinner, with lots of blank spaces for write-ins.

He knew that some bosses were scowling and frightening and ran a very tight ship, but he was optimistic, encouraging, loose with praise. He himself as a child had responded only to "positive reinforcement," as the psychologist at school had said, and just gave up if criticized; he assumed that being an employee was similar to being a child. He liked to think he could spot talent; in any event he was always "challenging" his young staff with tasks that were too hard for them but thrilled them to be trusted with. When they dressed well, he flattered them, though he knew flattery for women could seem problematic, even abusive. In any event he didn't know what was considered stylish these days.

At first he'd imagined he would have to do everything himself, but soon he discovered the joy of delegating. To do so he had to be very clear about what he wanted his staff to accomplish, and that meant thinking out every task in advance. Sometimes it was easier to do it himself. His favorite assistant was Sarah, a young black graduate from Wellesley whose father was an orthopedic surgeon. She had beautiful manners, she dressed well, she made the hand gestures of a Balinese dancer, her wrists pivoting as she talked. She was very thin. She said all white men were racist and all black men were sexist. Aldwych thought then she must be a lesbian. She was very good with her elders, who found her ardent and curious about everything. She read nonfiction, difficult books that explored the disasters of the day. Global warming was her favorite. She refused to have an air conditioner, she took very quick showers, she recycled the ash from her fireplace in cloth bags to wash her clothes, lots of soaking. She said the fashion industry was the world's biggest polluter; all her clothes were made to order after her own designs. She turned the scraps into quilts for the homeless and sometimes she spotted a beggar on the sidewalk sleeping under her own striped drugget pattern from Alaïa. August and Zaza dropped by, bringing their own brand of glamor and marked turnout; these visits plunged the boss into a giddy happiness never otherwise seen by his assistants.

· · ·

Aldwych claimed he'd never danced and couldn't even do the fox trot, which wasn't true since in fifth and sixth grades he'd taken classes in ballroom dancing and as an extra man he'd whirled across the marble floors some of Tuxedo Park's most visible debutantes. It's also where he'd had his first gay experiences. The paunchy president of the Bachelors' Cotillion had lured him up as a fifteen-year-old to his suite in the Roosevelt Hotel on Madison, where he got him drunk on Scotch, loosened his suspenders, and fell on the floor before his bare ass and gave him his first rim job. His subsequent kisses tasted of Johnnie Walker and unwiped bottom.

As a young teen, Aldwych spent hours and hours alone in his father's Princeton House on Brookstone Drive. The "staff" went home at night and his father usually stayed in Manhattan with his mistress, a painter on Bond Street who thought children were small, inferior adults though she declared them "adorable." In the big twelve-room house he liked to play a recording of Ravel's *Menuet antique* and leap about in the nude, all the lights extinguished. It was what he called "interpretive dance," and he would twirl and thump and stoop and jump, imagining how he looked naked with his muscular rump and still hairless torso, his penis too small to signify, his beardless face creamy to the touch. He always imagined an astonished observer, a clothed man sitting in the shadows, feverishly attentive.

He took his cue from the music, which he knew by heart. He would stand on his toes, lie briefly and lightly on his back on the sofa, fluttering his legs in *entrechats* in the air, stand suddenly and weave his hands in mystical

Oriental patterns, practice the Scottish sword dance he'd learned for a school production of *Brigadoon,* waltz an invisible partner around the room in giant, reeling steps, cling to the back of a chair in order to extend his right leg far, far behind him without losing his balance. He felt so free, so exalted, so pagan as he spun, crouched, leapt, imagining that his bluish-white body was exciting the imagined adult male observer in the shadows. He was intensely aware that he was beautiful, though "being beautiful" required a putative observer.

Veering headlights heralded his father's unexpected return. Aldwych doused the deafening music, climbed into his clothes, restored the furniture to its customary positions, flipped the rug back into place, wiped the sweat from his face, tried to catch his breath, switched on a lamp, and picked up a book. His father saw him from a room away and said "Time for bed, champ," before staggering drunkenly up the stairs. His father seemed in a bad mood; perhaps he'd quarreled with his "lady friend" once again. Aldwych wondered what his father would have thought if he'd caught his son interpreting us all in his splendid naked dance.

So Aldwych had a vivid memory of the expressiveness and ecstasy of dance; he hoped that August's training and technique only added to the boy's exaltation rather than professionalizing it out of existence. Once he got August to admit, though the boy had no vocabulary to express it, that he never felt so electric, so immanent, so much the object of so many minds at once as when he was dancing, that his groin and buttocks glowed from such rapturous attention, that he felt as if each note welling up from the orchestra was awakened by his magical tread on imaginary piano keys, that he was *making* the music rather than just responding to it. Then there was the spiritual side to dance, the feeling that it was timeless, that it connected us all with the Russian imperial court, that it was an expression of the soul through the body.

The brightening lights were dipping his body, as it were, into whiter and whiter solutions of cleansing vinegar and soda, dissolving the grime and patina until the original detail could be read even from the highest balcony as though freshly minted. He was new and shiny. He'd practiced so much that muscle memory guided him through these ten pirouettes into these twenty-two tours jetés, during which he never lost his visual spot, and went gliding down onto one knee into an open-armed, heavy-breathing, broadly smiling *bow*. He knew his moves so instinctively that he was convinced he brought nobility and elegance and masculinity to his role, that he wasn't just a one-trick pony but also a sensitive, feeling human being in complete mastery of every move and able to give meaning to his portrayal.

. . .

At the office, Aldwych had to make cold calls to rich people outside his circle. It was pure torture for him. He was asking them to put up serious money in exchange for just a handful of perks—having an early choice of seats, their names in the program, a meet-and-greet with the dancers, bad champagne in plastic flutes and rubbery supermarket brie, a chance to rub shoulders with other rich people, to wear couture, to invite new acquaintances to sit on *their* board for the Skowhegan art school in Maine or whatever. That organization in Maine was fully deductible, and they had a big annual dinner dance in New York and another prize dinner to recognize benefactors in the arts (Mrs. Ned Chase, Noelle de Jesus, one of the younger Pillsburys who spoke English with a French accent, one of the old Dutch elite, born van Zuylen but married to a Jew, Rephun, who'd planted half the trees subscribed in Hebron for firing the glassmaking kilns).

If Aldwych was lucky, the cold calls reached people who recognized his family name or were somehow connected to the microwave business or who came from Bernardsville or had attended Princeton, who'd gone to his sister's debut (more likely their parents had gone), who'd known his ex-wife, who'd studied ballet as little girls and had gone onstage in Balanchine's *Nutcracker*, who were the daughter-in-law of the family dentist, Bill Pifer, whose wife, Cathy, had been a Broadway hoofer, or who'd sailed in the Bermuda Cup on his great-uncle's boat, the *Pendennis*. People who didn't recognize his name or want to be in his circle (or even know he had a circle) could be very rude and paranoid. "Who is this? Ballet? I don't have any daughters. How did you get this number?"

It turned out that there were countless rich people in America who were nobodies and just enjoyed themselves riding around on their mowers and giving barbecues for their neighbors and employees. They made their money putting up ugly houses or owning a dry cleaning chain; they had no interest in "society," no desire to present their children to famous old names, didn't even know those names existed, preferred taking their whole extended family to Honolulu, all thirty-six members, for a week-long luau. His lawyer, Laurence, said you should approach some of these new tech zillionaires ("They're not all in California") who might want "naming privileges" for the concert hall you build and who you want to act like Maecenases and to meet the old New York white shoe elite, who at least know enough names to be impressed. One woman said, "Why don't you apply for grants? Why should I give you my hard-earned cash?"

. . .

Aldwych had beautiful if very casual manners. He was always cheerful, but didn't bray with laughter. He had learned gentlemen don't laugh. He was knowledgeable but never pedantic. With men who thought they were great, he was quick to admit their superiority, to chuckle over their jokes, to admire their insights and pay court to their wives (who were the ones who would decide whether you'd ever be invited back). Women were the social directors of America. Even Henry James in *The American Scene* noticed how the women were much superior to the men in his native country, which he was visiting for the first time in twenty years. More cultured, better hosts, better conversationalists—just more interesting. Aldwych knew how to take an interest in people without making them feel scrutinized. He was good at spotting people's secret vanities and might say, "The world might revere you as a great editor, but they don't know you could have been equally remarkable as a chef." Most editors anyway were only interested in famous cooks and their cookbooks, which had completely replaced literary fiction or memoir or biography or travel in their imagination (unless those genres could be squeezed into a cookbook).

He caught sight of himself and realized he needed a haircut; his neck was a thicket of gray brambles. And he'd put on five pounds nibbling hors d'oeuvres and constantly drinking.

. . .

He'd never spent so many evenings with the "wrong" people as he did now. He had no children who might invite vulgar or abusive guests into his well-heeled, soft-spoken world (children or unsuitable mates were usually the Trojan horse soldiers being sneaked into society's fortress). But if he'd been spared dubious company before, now he sought it out (as long as they were *rich* nobodies). He was invited to dull readings of amateur plays, to bas mitzvah parties on rented boats in the Hudson, to dinners in new restaurants seeking publicity that had given free entry to a lady with a huge Rolodex, to the launch of a new perfume in someone's rented "party space" in a Tenth Avenue loft where they served daiquiris and freshly shucked oysters, all meant to complement the scent, "Sea Mist." He'd never seen so many people he didn't know; it was like the wrong night at the opera, full of Russian thugs in black tie and their whores in gold slips. He realized that New York was a huge city of immense wealth and that all these anonymous millionaires had to go somewhere and be seen doing something; why couldn't they come to his ballet and have their names engraved on his orchestra seats?

He wondered if he should stop drinking. He was incapable of cutting down, but stopping altogether would be possible. But then he thought he wouldn't make the effort. He liked the way the first Scotch at five marked a transition from the day to the night. He also liked how a bedtime Scotch acted as a reward for all the ennuis of the day. He also liked how drink made the time pass flawlessly with nearly no transitions. It also unglued his tongue and made him join in on no matter what chatter was currently on tap. It gave him a new burst of energy. It rubbed away inhibitions and made him act out any fantasy immediately, no interval between thought and action, hesitation and outrage. It made him cordial and erased all boredom. Since he always felt just a bit guilty for being drunk, it made him apologetic and forbearing, whereas he could be crusty when sober.

No, he thought it was altogether better to stay drunk. Devious people liked it because they thought they could take advantage of a drinker; it emboldened them. And liquor had always been the engine for him to pursue love.

He thought, *How strange love is*, not love within the tribe but exogenous love, it can lead you into other languages, into eating arepas at a food stand covered with palm fronds in hundred-degree weather, into listening to an avant-garde opera in English in a Brooklyn studio, into making love to a go-go boy in a Queens apartment he shares with the bouncer from his club and lots of life-size statues of crowned Moors, into wondering how to escape from the shanty deep in a Bavarian forest. From August he'd learned the French Canadian word *frasil*, which meant "snow floating on water"; he'd learned s*audade*, "profound longing for someone," from a Brazilian twenty-two-year-old; from an Italian schoolboy he'd learned *barlume*, a "glimmer as seen through water," just as a Chinese scholar had taught him that *qi* refers to the breath that animates the universe.

Now love was causing him to spend so many evenings out with deplorables as he slowly put together the nut for his ballet company. He'd even engaged a financial planner to help him devise a budget for the first year, an astounding amount. He thought if he ate at home more he could save—insignificant amounts, anthills next to the looming mountain of his ballet budget, as large as the national debt of Uruguay.

He who'd been idle and cosseted all his life, who had been a B student and hadn't played sports, who'd married an undemanding wife, was childless—he'd somehow assumed that this was the baseline for all New Yorkers, maybe all Americans. On the evening news he heard about families living in their cars and frequenting food banks, but he assumed they'd been foolish, bred too many children, been stoned every day, hadn't finished high school, were just part of "the culture of poverty," regrettably hadn't learned English properly, hadn't taken their rich uncle's offer. It was clear that all these unfortunate people must have done something wrong; otherwise they'd be well fed and idle like him.

Or as he had been, before the ballet had swamped him in tedious detail and long lists of Things to Do Today, lists that he'd try to organize from most to least important and that he'd redraw every morning, recopying most of the unperformed items.

He tried to keep Dietrich "in the loop," abreast of his fundraising activities but quickly learned that his struggles were only disquieting to the choreographer, who was used to government subsidies. He decided to proceed with more confidence, less detail.

Meanwhile he'd grown slightly apart from August, the person he was doing all this for. Aldwych had to write himself notes to remind him to congratulate August on his good reviews from Howard Marks in the *Times*, to kiss him good night. Aldwych had begun to smoke and drink again and he worried that the cigarette smell would repulse the boy. But he didn't seem to notice it, even though that cabdriver that time had said to Aldwych, "You stink like an ashtray! Your clothes must be steeped in smoke."

He barely had a moment to talk to August. He awakened before August and kissed him on his taut stomach without ever disturbing his sleep. Sometimes after dinner with a rich vulgarian he'd sneak into the theater to see the third act of Stravinsky's *Symphony in Three Movements* with August and Zaza, winding itself up like a giant turbine. As often as not he'd nod off after their solos.

He'd suddenly ask himself why he bothered. August seemed happy with his position in the New York City Ballet; he was getting all the roles he wanted, which had been the original impetus for this ballet business. But the boy was stubborn about how he wanted to "renew" himself, make himself even more desirable by being daring. That's what the Ballets Russes did. He'd read about it. Nijinsky had choreographed *The Rite of Spring* and the audience had gotten into fistfights. Later, in *Afternoon of a Faun*, he'd lewdly made love to a scarf. In one ballet they'd danced to the sound of airplane propellers; in another they'd played tennis. Like a dragonfly who has only fifty days to live, he must do something remarkable with each one, something scandalous, something *new*.

Aldwych read the massive biography of Lincoln Kirstein and realized that he was almost always scrambling after money and that he would have to make up deficits out of his own ever lighter pockets. He was obviously a manic-depressive who had torrential energies depending on which pole he was visiting. But nowadays everyone spoke of Balanchine and Stravinsky but seldom of Kirstein himself; his efforts had been necessary but thankless. Moreover, Kirstein had been a childhood friend of Rockefeller and other rich, powerful men. His life was a cautionary tale. Kirstein at the end had stopped going out to dinner and starting ordering in Chinese.

When Aldwych discussed the new ballet company with August, the boy invariably looked sad and guiltily kept kissing Aldwych's eyelids. Aldwych loved the attention, but he couldn't help feeling that the sadness and guilt were ominous. Was August still all in on the project?

Rosita was steam-cleaning the bathroom where Pablo had drunkenly pissed on the floor the night before. Aldwych thought he must give her a raise, although she always protested about receiving more money. The gentle hiss of the steam reminded August of Pablo's disgraceful behavior. "Should I get rid of him?" August asked.

Aldwych appreciated being awarded this *droit de seigneur* from August. If he banished Pablo, he doubted that that would change anything, but it was polite of August to pretend it would. Pablo had told them he was "massaging" Ernestine these days, and August was both turned on by Pablo's renewed heterosexual adventures (when he sucked Pablo he liked to think where this cock had been) and felt freed by Pablo's "infidelity," which counted as more serious because it was with a woman. An affair with another boy he could take as child's play, innocent horny fumbling, while sex with a woman made everything grown-up, almost legal, something that would have life consequences. Aldwych was less impressed by women because he was more familiar with them. For him they were just random human beings grazing in search of love and excitement and status, just like men, like everyone. Maybe they were a bit elevated because they were more beautiful, modest, civilized, had greater self-control. Ernestine seemed to have loads of self-control. He wondered what Bryce must think of her "abuse" of a much younger man.

As the winter progressed, Aldwych watched his war chest get bigger and bigger. Laurence got him incorporated as a nonprofit and all contributions were tax deductible. As the year drew to a close, many of his old and new rich friends were urged by their accountants to make bigger and bigger contributions. Aldwych calculated that for every ten thousand dollars, he'd had to spend a night drunk with strangers. He could feel his health, his body deteriorating while August, lying beside him, became ever sleeker and more muscular. It was as if the life force were being transfused through transparent tubes from one body to the other. When Aldwych dragged himself to the theater to watch his protégé, he noticed more and more that the audience was made up of the old and the lame, with crippled people, morbidly obese people, "all there"? to worship at the fountain of youth, physical perfection, and daring (Zaza had said, "I know I'm dancing well when I'm always slightly frightened—will he catch me, lift me, support me?"). It was like the flushed, sweating, soused ancient Romans all crowded into the Colosseum to watch their lithe, trained slaves fight each other to the death. Just as all these deformed masses cheered and clapped for the exquisite Zaza and the flawless August, so the Roman rabble had been sober (or drunk) enough to hoot for their favorite gladiators. Just as the enslaved Abyssinians or Gauls threw their metal nets over the advancing, starving lions, so the dancers beguiled their fans with ever more dizzying leaps, ever more perilous turns. The grotesque public were seated; the performers were on their pointed feet and more and more active in their death-defying games.

Or it was like Lourdes.

At the intermission Aldwych always downed three vodkas. No more bad champagne. Maybe he was too disheveled, or smelled bad, but his kindly seat partner snubbed him now; had he gone too far in his dissolution?

She looked right through him as if he were a ghost; she did not hear his comments or questions. Whenever he spoke she turned away toward her wizened girlfriend. More and more, August slept in his own bed with the noisy, raucous Pablo. Aldwych hoped that constant buggering wouldn't feminize August's body, widen his hips, shrink his balls; August must give at least onstage the impression of pure masculinity. It wasn't healthy to be flooded with another man's semen.

At last, by January, Aldwych had squirreled away enough money to reserve two weeks of Dietrich's time and that of his company. He'd put them in the Koch in the summer two years hence when the New York City Ballet was out of town. Aldwych had to advance a considerable sum to block out those two weeks—transportation, all the salaries of the dancers and the backstage people, Dietrich's personal fee, a down payment on hotel rooms for the troupe. Although Aldwych never hinted that his plans for inviting the company to New York were conditional, the unspoken truth was that the New York reviews would determine their future tours. If they were spectacular (as Twyla Tharp's had been, or Mark Morris's, or Justin Peck's), that *succès d'estime* would sweep away all hesitation on every side, including the investors'.

. . .

Ernestine enjoyed playing with Pablo, especially when she thought that that cock had been up August's hole.

She kept bringing him to her room at the Pierre. He would always bring her off at least three times (he'd added cunnilingus to his repertory). Once, when she'd asked him if he ever sucked August, he'd pointed out to her that he was a real man and would never touch another man's genitals, though to be fair, a bisexual friend of his had said sucking cock was like licking pussy on a stick.

She couldn't understand why she was turned on by gay men. On Pornhub she would select MFM porno, two men and a woman, but if the men fucked only the woman she'd lose interest. One video she liked the most and kept returning to showed a man taking turns fucking another man, then a woman, then back to the man, his alternating strokes establishing an equivalence between asshole and cunt. Then he started switching from the guy's mouth to the woman's asshole.

Maybe her taste for MFM sex had to do with her own sadism. She liked humiliating Bryce (in fact it was the only kind of sex they had, and then only when they were both drunk). She had never fucked a man with a strap-on but the idea appealed to her. When she was a kid at a private little-girls' school she would make the other students sneak out of their houses one of their father's belts, which she would whip them with. The other girls fell right in line; no one ever questioned her right to subject them to her outrageous caprice.

Or maybe she liked the idea of a woman humiliating a man with the help of a male assistant. She cherished the idea of feminizing a male victim, of getting him to wear silk panties and an empty bra hugging his shaved chest, of putting his penis in a locked cage and a big butt plug up his ass, of growing his hair long and dying it blond. She liked the idea of cuckolding pitiful little Bryce with a real man like Pablo, forcing him to observe his wife's subjection to a virile young man. Imaginative as she was, and stimulated by pornography (admittedly, she preferred written porno to films), she still thought she had much to learn from the right mentor.

Everyone by definition thinks his own taste is the best in the world, but most people suspect they have much to learn in mastering a skill (such as sadism). She knew that most sadists began their training as masochists, but she agreed with the French philosopher Deleuze that sadism and masochism were not opposites but entirely separate pathologies. She herself had never wanted to be hurt or dominated, but her juices ran when she could make someone else sob or shout. She liked outshining other people, even if it was beyond their understanding. She loved wearing the latest fashions and then insisting she'd bought them at a charity sale. She liked mispronouncing a word in the same way the guest of honor had done, though everyone else could see through her polite ruse. She liked calling an actor Olivier, though his name was Oliver. When someone washed their grapes in the finger-bowl she did the same. She worked lines from a poet's work into the conversation, though no one suspected her of her hidden compliment. Once when someone's ill-behaved basset had tried to scratch his way up the table to the food and the host had nearly fainted, she'd lifted the dog and put him at the very center of the table ("The poor frustrated darling, now he's where he belongs"). She claimed she couldn't really play the piano, then reeled off a note-perfect Scarlatti sonata but broke it off near the end saying she couldn't remember it.

She thought again of dominating August. She was enamored of that slap-hungry ass, that pale perfection that begged to be red. By those golden raisin nipples, that longed to be bruised to become juicy purple grapes. But that was all to come in the distant future.

And the truth was that Pablo had no conversation; he knew nothing of her world and didn't understand its delicate maneuvering. Whereas she believed that August, because he was an artist and had been polished by his months of living with Aldwych (and his own extraordinary powers of observation), would be the ideal companion, a friend in the salon and a victim in the boudoir.

Now her only job was to wrest him away from the pointless Aldwych, who was as ineffectual as his nephew Bryce. Good thing they were the last of the Wests—they were incapable of everything, *negati in tutto*, as the Italians might say . . . Once she had control over August, he would be lovely to spoil (and to humiliate). She longed to violate his hole.

She'd been reluctant to discuss her sadism with her Jungian analyst, fearing that therapy might make it go away, but she was proud of it; it was a crucial part of her identity. She wanted to talk about it. Ever since she'd beaten the girls with their fathers' belts she'd experienced a hot flush of pleasure with every aggression. Her only fear was that it would get out of control and she wouldn't be able to contain it. Only with time and endless episodes with her absurd husband had she been able to master her enthusiasm. Now she knew exactly when to pull back before drawing blood. One of her slaves had complained after the fact, however, that she wasn't tender enough postsession. Though she really did despise her victims, she'd learned to conceal her disgust and hold them and be kind after the brutalities. Since her shrink had taken an oath of the confessional, at last she felt free to brag about her sadistic acts and enjoyed making him appear slightly shocked, even awkward. Despite his surprise, he did see her sadism as the fulfillment of her imago, the necessary opposite of her society-bred sweetness, the animus lurking within the anima. She had been schooled for years into politeness; roughing someone up felt so freeing, like breaking an aunt's treasured Venetian glass into a hundred shards.

12

E rnestine talked Pablo into inviting August to an afternoon of pain and pleasure at the Pierre. August didn't need much persuading. He'd never had successful sex with a woman and was curious whether he'd be able to keep an erection and perform normally. That Pablo would be present he found reassuring, since he feared most disappointing the woman and leaving her frustrated and bitter.

At first he watched Pablo take Ernestine on while he propped himself up on one elbow, then began to kiss Ernestine, whose lips tasted of the apricot she'd just eaten. Then he touched her breasts and she grabbed his ridiculous nipples. She positioned herself so that she could embrace him more deeply while Pablo continued rogering her. Her left hand fluttered past August's penis, which they both noticed with delight was rigid. As soon as Pablo climaxed, she pulled herself free and sat on August's lap. He liked the idea that she was full of Pablo's cum, which was rancid, cloudy, and syrupy, as August well knew.

August was thrilled with his ability to perform heterosexually and felt a surge of gratitude to Ernestine, as if she alone held the key to his success with women, though he'd obtained his success under admittedly special circumstances. He wondered if he'd be able to stay erect without Pablo's connivance. In any event he felt such tenderness toward Ernestine, though she was his mother's age (Ernestine was in much better shape, and a recent facelift had erased all of her lines, though it had left her looking a bit butchered, with startled eyes, a paralyzed cheek, and a mouth that couldn't quite close). All three of them thought it had been a wonderful afternoon.

August walked briskly up Fifth Avenue with Pablo, chatting about cool, inconsequential things but feeling that a ring of fire, a burning curse, had flickered out. He'd always resented men with their hairy balls in his face, their horrible genitals probing his mouth, testing his gag reflex, their dry wide fingers invading his tender anus. He hated their smells and excessive saliva and rotten farts, their rectum breath, the odor of the night's pesto, their stupid way of saying "Fuck! Fuck! Fuck!" again and again as if it expressed anything. Even so, it was better than being someone's son or father or bitch or cunt, than being told the older man was getting his boy "pregnant" and he, the little wife, must keep his babies in his asshole till dawn.

He was sure women could be disgusting too, but Ernestine had magically made him a member of the human race. He felt he'd lost his "interesting" accent overnight and no longer needed to explain where he was from and how he'd learned the new language so well. He was no longer an easy, repetitious talking point but had become as mysterious and ordinary as anyone else. He no longer needed to pretend he found children undesirable; now he could sire them. He no longer had to do facial isometrics and bathe his skin in cream; he no longer had to be beautiful and young. He could age and watch his hair recede with equanimity. He didn't have to keep his voice low; his bigger balls would see to that. On stage he could pretend to be a prince in a classic ballet; that was all the pretending that was required of him. Looking with love at the ballerina would now be convincing; he hoped he'd have many children that would resemble him.

. . .

Ernestine pretended to August that she adored his mother, so sweet and companionable. She said she couldn't bear to think of that adorable woman shivering in the Canadian winter and wanted her to come down to Palm Beach for January; they'd be flown down in her private jet. August was so enthralled by Ernestine after his "success" with her that he thought his mother's visit to Palm Beach was a great idea. Marthe herself was less enthusiastic. She didn't have the right clothes. She couldn't leave her husband alone; he couldn't cook and he'd starve to death. And how would Ernestine and she communicate? And why should she want her company? And Marthe was afraid of airplanes; she'd never flown.

Ernestine had an answer for everything. The clothes would be her discards from when she was heavier (a white lie, since she'd never been heavy). She would order two weeks of Fresh-to-Go prepared-and-delivered meals for the husband. She would fly Marthe to New York on the travel points she'd saved (not true, she never bothered with "miles.") And she'd hired a French Canadian cook, very discreet, who could translate.

It all worked as planned. Marthe was grateful to escape the cold and luxuriate among the terrace geraniums in her new large navy blue swimsuit. The two French Canadians liked each other on first sight; they were from neighboring villages (Lazarette was from Carte du Tendre). Ernestine had instructed Lazarette to quiz Marthe about her son and to suggest he was being "exploited" by the toxic Aldwych, both as a star-to-be of this foreign, dubious company when he was already a principal of the world's greatest ballet company and as a sex partner to a hopeless old predator, whereas Ernestine had whispered that she had firsthand knowledge that August was "normal," even better than average if given the chance. Within a day, hostess and guest were discussing, in their impressionist French, Aldwych's terrible predation. When Marthe asked Ernestine directly if she had proof of her boy's normality, Ernestine lowered her eyes modestly in confirmation.

Ernestine fluttered like a butterfly in her yellow muumuu watering the flowers. It was a cool, sunny day, and down below, the breakers gleamed like freshly whipped meringue. Marthe asked, "What are those things growing there? I've never seen them before."

"Palms. Palm trees. Aren't they lovely?"

That was the level of their very intermittent conversation, unless Ernestine could think of a new angle to unsettle August's friendship with Aldwych, whereupon she was galvanized into a sustained effort of bad French. "Of course Aldwych is my husband's uncle and I hate to be disloyal to him. Only in an emergency like this and for dear friends like August and my dear Marthe would I sound the alarm. But I'm so afraid that that immoral man—*la main au collet*—would destroy the career of the world's greatest (but most naïve) dancer, and all just to gain a greater hold over his innocent flesh, though I know intimately that Eddie is not like that (*comme ça*)."

"Oh!" Marthe exclaimed, waving away a big bee that had somehow, despite the breeze, flown way up to the terrace. She took another sip of her iced sweet lemon tea. "I wish I could phone him right now. But isn't long distance too expensive?"

"Too expensive? Miraculously, it's no longer dear. But shouldn't you wait till you can talk this through in person in New York, when you return all healthy and energetic from your all-fruit diet and lightly tanned? Remember how his too-kind heart has attached him to that exploiting Aldwych. Although he's my uncle, I think he has the power of the devil. Let's see what your daily passage of the Holy Bible tells you:

> Jesus said: "Alas for you, scribes and Pharisees, you hypocrites! You who shut up the kingdom of heaven in men's faces, neither going in yourselves nor allowing others to go in who want to.
>
> "Alas for you, scribes and Pharisees, you hypocrites! You who travel over sea and land to make a single proselyte, and when you have him you make him twice as fit for hell as you are."

Marthe looked a bit confused but simultaneously reassured by the familiar-sounding gibberish.

"See how poor August is the single proselyte whom Aldwych has seduced and made fit for hell? We're not talking just about a great career but also about an immortal soul. But of course I would do nothing to persuade you. He is or was your innocent son. Though Aldwych is preparing his one convert for eternal damnation. Oh, Marthe, if only you could save him!"

They discussed Marthe's best strategy while the heavenly zephyrs blew against their brown cheeks and Marthe was encouraged to try her first Bloody Mary (possibly her first tomato juice).

"Do you think ballet is the devil's work?" Marthe asked in her slurred French after her third drink.

"Why would you think that?"

"We see way up the woman's legs even to her nether lips. And we see that big bulge in the man's crotch *et son beau cul*, and those are images of desire. The music is very captivating, the dancing is by turns feverish and languishing, the man is constantly touching, twirling, and lifting the scarcely clad woman, which can't be right."

"But beautiful?"

"Yes, that's how you know it's sinful. Men are seduced by long legs, slender, athletic bodies, extreme youth. That's why my husband, Roger, and I are so pleased we're both chubby and past the breeding age."

"That must be a consolation," Ernestine said with big sober eyes contradicted by her gay smile. Her half-paralyzed face was hard to read.

The next day, tanned and hung over and full of resolve, the ladies headed back in the private plane to New York. Before they left, Lazarette prepared a respectable poutine, though she couldn't find the cheese curds in Palm Beach and had to substitute shredded mozzarella. Marthe looked down on the wind-scuffed ocean and the palms shaking their heads like women after a shower. She had tears in her eyes; it had been not only the best but also the only vacation in her life. She knew people went on vacation, even came to Canada on vacation for some reason, but it wasn't for poor people like Roger and her. After a moment she recalled Christ's promise that the poor shall inherit the earth (*les pauvres hériteront la terre*) and smiled with satisfaction, though she wondered what she would do with it all.

. . .

Aldwych had befriended August's dresser, chatted him up, tipped him experimentally, and finally bribed him to hand over a pair of August's unwashed practice tights, which Aldwych slept beside every night when August himself wasn't in the bed. And hid every morning under his stockings. Aldwych thought how lucky he was to possess this much of the sacred boy, his *puer eternus*, who with any luck would remain eternally young if Aldwych had anything to do with it. Though how he'd purchase eternal youth for someone—that he hadn't quite figured out.

The less he actually touched the boy the more he fetishized him. He'd hoard a half apple that was rich with the even marks of August's new teeth. Or he'd visit August's bathroom when it was still ripe with the odor of August's shit. Or he'd quickly inhale the life-giving properties of some just-discarded underpants, down to the brown seam in the fabric. He'd rustle through his sheets feeling for starchy patches before declaring disappointedly, *"Pas de sperme ici."*

He collected publicity shots of August, spread them out on his bed, and, as he thought of it, "wallowed" in them as he tried to elicit an orgasm. He daydreamed about holding the boy from behind, his hands striking the xylophone of his abdominals. Or he imagined engulfing with his mouth the solid uncut penis, his tongue glistening over the exposed meatus. Or he opened his arms as his angel floated down on top of him and Aldwych's flabby arms enclosed the slender perfection.

One afternoon Pablo surprised him by knocking on the front door. It was a loud, solid knock, and Aldwych wondered how the person slipped past the doorman without being announced. When he heard Pablo's name he opened immediately; was he here to rendezvous with August? As soon as he entered, he took Aldwych's right hand between both of his. His skin was warm as an afternoon brick and just as rough. And grateful to the touch.

"Whassup?" he asked in that confounding way of the young.

Aldwych replied as August had taught him, "Not much. It's so great to see you, but I'm afraid August isn't here."

"I came to see you."

"What a lovely surprise. Come into the sitting room."

"No, your room."

"Of course," Aldwych said on a note of puzzlement.

When they'd secreted themselves in the bedroom, Pablo pulled him down beside him on the edge of the bed. "Ernestine. Do you know about her and August? I think you might wanna know."

"No. I didn't even know they were anything more than vague acquaintances."

"To cut to the chase, I had a three-way with her and August."

"I'm astonished!" Aldwych was also a bit thrilled.

"Yeah, but that's not what I'm getting at. I think they're still seeing each other—without me."

Aldwych was amused by Pablo's adorable wounded vanity. "But I thought Ernestine was in Florida."

"She got back Monday. She was down there with Marthe, August's mother."

Aldwych looked at Pablo as a child might look at a magician, wondering what else might come out of the top hat. "And did the Chinaman go to the moon?"

"Huh?" Pablo looked at him strangely. "Don't get all whoo-hoo on me." He sketched a spiral in the air beside his head. "No, I think it's bad for August. You and I must save him against that woman. She's really a witch. I'm afraid she'll—" he searched for the word—"steal his soul. We say that in Spanish."

"I didn't realize August was attracted to women."

A different, softer look came over Pablo's face. "You're really a nice guy. And so good for August." Pablo took both of Aldwych's hands in both of his.

A moment later Pablo had taken his hard uncut penis out of his pants and Aldwych was staring it in the eye. August was uncircumcised as well, but whereas unveiling the head of *his* penis was like brushing aside a mask to reveal the thing's true identity, Pablo's drooling head remained in its foreskin like a large animal that had taken refuge in a well and probably would stay there.

It felt exciting and a little transgressive to be "cheating" on August, although he knew he, Aldwych, had no claims on the boy and August himself couldn't care less about Pablo's purely theoretical constancy. It was thrilling to be promoted into August's and Pablo's erotic company, if only for ten minutes, but there was also someone missing: August. Of course they'd had their spit-roasting threesome, but Pablo had singled him out this time—why, he wondered.

After Pablo had filled Aldwych's mouth with cum, Aldwych swallowed it but thought it a bit sacrilegious— partly because he was stealing sperm that belonged to August and partly because Aldwych felt he was somehow being "untrue" to his beloved boy.

In his incoherent, indignant way, Pablo began to impugn Ernestine for seducing the virginal August.

"But how did he end up there in her claws?" Aldwych felt childlike and respectful because Pablo was holding his boneless, liver-spotted hand in both of his fleshy brown paws, warm with youth.

Pablo shrugged as if he couldn't be bothered with such details but at last admitted that he had been persuaded by Ernestine to invite him over to an orgy at the Pierre.

"The Pierre!" Aldwych sputtered irrelevantly. "Why ever was she receiving at the Pierre?" The place made him more indignant than the act.

"What's so special about the Pierre?"

"Why should any New Yorker rent a hotel room?"

"Maybe she has lots of guys come up there."

"Ernestine is really becoming preposterous."

"You're telling me," Pablo said doubtfully.

Aldwych looked at Pablo as of a different species, someone you could technically have sex with but the union would be sterile; the chromosomes just didn't match up, some overlap but no identical sequencing.

Pablo explained how he had been willing to share August with Ernestine once or twice but now she was replacing him entirely. Sure, at first they had had a few three-ways. Ernestine studied how Pablo kept a finger stuck up August's ass. "He really likes that, doesn't he?" she'd asked when August was taking a leak. "Maybe if I played with his ass too, he'd stay hard. Do you think that was Wallis Simpson's secret? Did she stick a finger up the king's ass?"

They were always together whenever August wasn't in rehearsal. They were constantly holed up in the Pierre eating chicken sandwiches (which couldn't be good for a dancer, Pablo thought; a dancer needed steak) or plunging out at night up the Taconic Parkway, trying to outrace the rain (which was dangerous, especially when August was behind the wheel, he who'd learned to drive on a tractor, not in a Ferrari). August looked exhausted all the time, trying to satisfy that nympho ("Even I couldn't keep up wid huh, a real man like me)."

Aldwych detached himself from Pablo, as if he couldn't think clearly as long as he was physically in contact with the young torero. "Can we back up for a moment? Why is Ernestine bothering herself with Marthe? They have nothing in common, including language. I'm sure Ernestine has something up her sleeve; what's her motive?"

"I guess her husband is just a pitiful little thing—and I'm too much a man for her."

"Wait," Aldwych said. "You met Bryce?"

"Several times." His eyes slid to one side. "The last time, Ernestine brought him in on a leash and made him kiss my ass."

"Oh, who can possibly enjoy those games?"

"The dude had a hard-on."

"But does she want August?"

"August must be just right."

"Except he's gay."

"He says he was just talked into being gay like that other dancer, whatchamacallit, Nijinsky, and he's always wanted to be straight."

"Hmm, with a woman his mother's age?"

"Why don't you and I become a thing? That would freak them out."

"That's a thought. But how could you go from a beauty like August to . . . me? Revenge isn't usually a solid basis for a relationship. Don't you think August is really gay? He seems such a bottom—some of his dance friends call him 'Greedy Glutes.'"

"August isn't so beautiful. He's too skinny. And his ass is always dirty. And I like people who are good people, like you. You're good people." Pablo liked the sound of that and he clung to it, as the ancient Greeks did to the syllogism. "You're good people in my opinion." He thought for a moment. "That's my definition of someone who says he's *versatile*. A bottom who doesn't douche."

Pablo came in slowly for a kiss, which he augmented with his square, slippery tongue. Aldwych felt intimidated by this massive block of a man, like one of those stones used to deny access to a pyramid's hidden riches. Yes, his body functioned as a stop to—rather than an invitation to—intimacy. His arms were massive, his chest was thick, even his wrists could not be circled. His neck was as wide as his head and big veins or muscles were quietly feeding his whole torso. Suddenly Aldwych could feel a finger as wide as a giant *maccherono* probing his ass. This anal insertion seemed completely at odds with the swooning, romantic look on Pablo's face; he kissed Aldwych ardently, and the old man felt utterly unprepared for this moment—his anus too tight from neglect, "dirty" possibly, his mouth sour, his dick as limp as (again) pasta past the al dente stage, overcooked, his body flabby and not washed recently enough, the pores on his nose too big and black, the hair sprouting out of his ears deafening, the liver spots covering his hands in full, ominous bloom.

And yet he didn't want to shy away foolishly like a spinster from this magnificent man who'd enjoyed his August so frequently, so carelessly. He didn't want to lose this one big chance to make love to a real player. Aldwych knew that in the eyes of the world he himself was the player, a winner with his pedigree and fortune and entrée, but of course if they were both undraped, Pablo would outclass him in every pair of desiring eyes. It was strange how beauty and youth and dick size trumped wealth, culture, kindness, and all the other virtues, though no one admitted it. We pretend we like the civilized and the good, but our thermometers measure only physical heat. We bend to the will of the rich or titled or famous, but only intermittently; we want to go home with the camel boy, not the overweight, overperfumed sheikh.

Pablo had bared his big chest, as glowing and muscular as a horse's. His darting, viscous tongue had hypnotized Aldwych, who felt himself giving in more and more to this young man. He was enjoying what August must relish four times a week. Aldwych knew he himself wasn't much—a scrawny pullet, not a prize hen—but even so the gods were accepting him as a modest offering. He was the impoverished juggler performing for Our Lady, casting balls in the air because that was the only thing he knew how to do.

Unexpectedly, Pablo liked to cuddle. Since Aldwych was so in love with August, he found the constant contact with another body intolerable. August had never snuggled, though occasionally in sleep he'd thrown an unintentional arm across Aldwych's scrawny body. He and August were parallel dreamers with no real hope for intersection. Each "cultivated his solitude" as Rilke recommended, knowing solitude was the inevitable human condition if invariably an ache, though an ache less painful than total isolation-tank deprivation.

Although Pablo said he didn't mind Aldwych's snoring, Pablo in truth was the epic snorer. He recognized that if his bedmate were his beloved August, he would enjoy his nocturnal proximity and the gentle roar of his breathing, that in fact he would press closer, hoping to be rewarded with an involuntary erection between his buttocks and a smelly breeze on his nape, the hypnotic pulse of the noisy, reassuring uvula.

But it was this horrid snuggling he detested. Soon Aldwych was precariously perched on the edge of the mattress, but even there, on the farthest reaches of his territory, Pablo was encroaching once more.

And Pablo kept telling him he loved him. Aldwych, who liked to think of himself as starved for affection, pushed Pablo angrily away and sputtered, "What am

I supposed to do with that? I may be the first man in history to complain about a declaration of love, but I feel it's so manipulative."

Pablo said, "I'm not asking for anything. It's just a feeling I have."

"I feel we're two schoolgirls. What an ungrateful wretch I am to reject—"

"You're not the first fellow to complain about that. I may come on too strong . . ."

At that moment the door swung open, a lozenge of ceiling light threw itself across the bed, August was standing there in shocking silhouette, Pablo raised himself on one intricately tattooed arm and said sheepishly, "Hey!" and August beat a hasty retreat, closing the door definitively.

Pablo lay back down and started cuddling again as if nothing worth mentioning had happened.

Aldwych hated him and jerked himself out of his muscular embrace, which reeked of a mildewed axillary odor.

Aldwych wanted to rush down the hall and climb into bed with August. By all rights they were meant to be bed partners. He belonged to August. He was aware of all the ironies of feeling the property of a man who had touched him only inadvertently, whereas he was allergic to this other big loving brute and his infernal cuddling. Gay life was so strange; he and Pablo should be rivals but constituted just one more odd couple.

The next morning he complained to a brainy friend about the cuddling and declarations of love, who rewarded him with this typed-out passage from William Gass:

> *Ich liebe dich.* No sentence pronounced by a judge could be more threatening. It means that you are about to receive a gift you may not want. It means that someone is making it very easy for you to injure them—if they are not making it inevitable—and in that way controlling your behavior. It means that someone wants you as an adjunct to their life. It means that they can survive, like mistletoe or moss, only on the side where the rib was removed. It means that one way or other they intend to own you. "Let me give you a hug. I have a hundred arms." So has Siva.

. . .

Marthe phoned August. She said she was in New York staying in Ernestine's room at the Pierre. "It's the most beautiful, elegant hotel you've ever seen. The chicken sandwiches are crustless, there are chandeliers even in the hallways—"

"*Arrête de te la peter,*" August joked in their dialect ("Stop showing off"), which made his mother giggle because *peter* also meant "fart."

They gossiped for a while. She told him that his father was furious she'd taken off for Florida.

"He doesn't understand anything."

"That's what I think."

His mother asked him to take her out to lunch. "I want to see one New York restaurant before I leave in two days. Not too expensive. But nice."

He promised to come by and pick her up at the Pierre at one thirty the next day. His mother said, *"Attache ta tuque,"* which meant "Hold on tight."

. . .

Then he called the Café Luxembourg and made a reservation. He wondered if the same arrogant waiter would be there.

His mother looked unusually stylish. He preferred her dowdy. She was thinner and was wearing makeup. He told her she looked "super."

After they'd ordered she told him how sweet Ernestine had been with her and the next time she was in Florida she'd think about going into the ocean if the waves weren't too big and the sharks weren't sighted.

"But how did you talk to each other?"

"I know a little English," Marthe said defensively, but she didn't. She told him about Lazarette and the mozzarella poutine. "Ernestine told me you and she have become inseparable."

"I adore her. She's so . . . tender," August confessed.

After the chilled watermelon and gazpacho soup ("Too spicy," Marthe said), she flattened her cloth napkin and said, "Ernestine is worried that Old-witch is destroying your career. I have a bad feeling about that man." She trembled as if a ghost had just crossed her path. "A very bad feeling."

August snapped, "My career is just fine."

"Now, maybe. Ernestine and I are coming to see you tonight."

"Marvelous. But what do you mean by 'now'? You've never taken an interest in my career before."

"That's not true! How can you say that?"

"It's the simple truth. Put your napkin back in your lap. People are looking."

That had always been a worry of theirs—what total strangers would think of them.

Marthe complied and said, "I just mean you're famous now but liking men will damage your reputation. And why does Old-witch want to put you in that obscure French dance company?"

Her words riled August—perhaps because she was speaking his original tongue, the heart's language; English never really reached him. "You and Ernestine should stay away from things you don't understand. Do you think Nureyev's sexuality damaged his career?"

"Who, dear?"

. . .

The salade niçoise with the salmon arrived. After a bite, Marthe said, "Too much vinegar."

Her complaints irritated him, though she'd always been this way. He said, "Besides, I'm not leaving the New York City Ballet. I just haven't found a way to tell Aldwych yet."

August lowered his head and Marthe smiled to herself. "I just have this feeling about him." She knew that "feeling" was a word in English and that no one could take exception to it.

When the profiteroles arrived, Marthe said, "The chocolate is not the best, and it's not hot enough, and the biscuits are soggy. But the ice cream is correct."

"And his name is not Old-witch." At that moment he saw the hateful waiter, who was undoubtedly heading their way to ask how their meal was going and might there be a Drambuie in the works? He must not have gotten the Visionworks gig.

13

Marthe reported back to Ernestine. "The restaurant wasn't much. Supposedly French cuisine. The profiteroles were soggy. But my big news is that August is not moving to Biarritz."

"Hurray!" She smiled. Ernestine had some of her fire-engine-red lipstick smeared on the upper right incisor. "And Aldwych? Did he say anything about him?" Her face was frozen in a misleading expression of awe—surgical, not inspired.

"No, but we'll work on him, now you've arranged for me to phone him from Canada."

Ernestine patted her hand abstractedly.

Marthe said, "You know you're always welcome to stay with us in Canada. It may not be as restful as Paume Bitch."

"Paume Bitch is very restful. Your husband might not like a visitor."

"Je m'en fous." Pause. "So tell me—is my son very virile? I'm not sure I should be asking that. We country people don't know what we can say."

"Yes, you do. You have exquisite manners. As to your question: Yes. Very virile. But I may be too old for him."

Marthe made an unmistakable blowing sound, as if the very thought of age in this case was absurd. "A real lady like you is . . . sans age."

"He does seem so . . . cozy and happy with me. But how long can that last? As I approach my climacteric? How long does anything last?" Ernestine wondered if Marthe knew what that word meant for a woman.

"Climate change! *Changement climatique.* That's all anyone talks about these days, though our winters are just as rude as they ever were, as *grossier.* And the summers? *La canicule.*"

Ernestine didn't attempt to explain, knowing the limits of her French vocabulary. She remembered that Roland Barthes had said talk of the weather as agreeable or not was a city dweller's topic. Country people spoke only of good or bad growing conditions, too much or too little rain, a sudden blast of cold. For them the weather was practical, not picturesque.

Ernestine was grateful she no longer had periods. They'd always shown up at inconvenient moments, like an unwelcome cousin who honks at the door at the wrong time and reveals the humble side of one's family. She met

August in her room in the Pierre. August, the darling, was always five minutes early.

Luckily he drank martinis, which she'd convinced him every civilized man imbibed before eating his chicken sandwich. She played a game with him that with every sip of his seriously incapacitating drink he must remove another article of clothing (each sock counted as one item), but at the end he must not take off his underwear. She had a rule that the first two times they played together they were not allowed to touch their partner's nor their own genitals nor wriggle out of their undies. Unbeknownst to August, a sex therapist acquaintance of hers whom she'd met once in Vegas had told her that that was the best cure for impotence—to allow arousal but forbid sex. It removed all "performance anxiety," apparently. It was as if you permitted an anguished pianist to dress, to enter to applause, to sit before his instrument but never touch the keys, or touch them without striking them. That was the best cure for stage fright. She was allowed to touch, even stroke, his erection through cloth but never allow him to ejaculate. His copious precum soaked through. He begged her to release him. But she was very firm about the terms of her therapy. He was told that on their third date he could undrape completely. That day he was half an hour late to the Pierre (something about a new Italian cobbler for the company).

. . .

Aldwych had laughed and laughed over Pablo's story about Ernestine forcing Bryce to kiss the boy's ass. A few days later, before he had to make a cold call to a foundation that frightened him and he had to rehearse several times, he punched in Bryce's number just for a laugh. They chatted for a while about an ailing aunt they were both neglecting, then Aldwych said, "I guess our Ernestine is off on several adventures . . ."

"What are you referring to? You are always so imprecise, Aldwych, it's hard to converse with you."

"I heard she made you kiss Pablo's ass," Aldwych enunciated carefully.

"Which I thoroughly enjoyed, both her commands and the act itself." He took in a little gasp of air. "I know you don't give a rat's ass what I think, but I've always considered the male heterosexual ass something we neglect unjustly. It is the grand portal to the soul and is the 'seat' of all the sentiments. Men are ashamed to admit they have rectal needs. As children they retain their feces until their mothers are obliged to administer repeated enemas. Boys deliberately irritate their fathers until, exploding with rage, their progenitors must take a lash to their tender, quivering behinds, 'the land never touched by the sun.' Sterile, unfruitful. As we grow older into our first manhood we feel an increasing need for invasive Korean massage. The clever masseur, who wants return business and is eager to attract a faithful clientele, finds himself dipping into the proverbial honey pot. Just a swipe here, a caress there, a deep lingering indentation into the rising, living dough. Of course there are the addicted adepts of elective surgery, always coaxing the odd hemorrhoid into early, operable prominence. Then there are those who insist their heroin habit has stalled their peristalsis, which can be relaunched only by deep irrigations of the bowel. I have a friend in Chicago, a bookseller, who proudly claims that his lover, always crowned with a motorcycle helmet to disguise his identity (he is a banker by day), is the porn star known as Master Traffic Cone since he can sit on an entire orange obstacle. The bookseller and the banker are frequent visitors to the remote Norman resort La Fistère."

"My, my," Aldwych muttered admiringly. "I didn't realize you were so engaged by rectal rights!"

. . .

Aldwych decided to invite August along in the car to see the "ruins of his childhood," by which he meant the site of his old family mansion just ten miles outside Princeton, a once famous estate that was now being leveled by a development company in order to turn the extensive grounds into ten McMansions. 'I've sold the property to build up our equity for the ballet company. I just thought you'd like to see my past before it's plowed under."

"Would it—Oh, I don't know how to ask this—"

"What is it?"

"Could Ernestine join us?"

"I thought you saw her every day. This was going to be a special occasion for just us. She already knows Joining Waters by heart."

"Joining . . . ?"

"That was the name of our estate. She played there every day as a child."

"She says she didn't know you as a child, that you were already an adolescent when she was born, that she didn't meet you till decades later."

"Well, never contradict a lady when she's inventing her past or discussing her age."

"So, can she come?"

"Of course she can. You make the arrangements."

Aldwych was deeply disappointed, but all three of them put a good face on it and were cheerful and kept exclaiming how much fun they were having.

August seldom got out of town except on tour. His time was so unvarying and regulated (class, rehearsal, performance) that he didn't feel right if he wasn't stretched out and exhausted, bruised or bleeding somewhere.

Ernestine suggested she sit in the back with August and that Aldwych sit in front with the chauffeur. ("That way you can give him directions"). She kept her nails, painted with a yellow shellac like a supermarket cashier's, firmly planted on August's muscular thigh. A ruby as big as a robin's egg glinted on her bony fingers. "My jewels wear me out," she said, slipping the ring into her purse. Aldwych wondered if she had cancer.

"Now this is the village where I grew up," Aldwych said, but Ernestine was murmuring something and August was laughing. "That was Mister Greenleaf's grocery store back in my day."

Ernestine asked, "Were you saying something, Aldwych?"

"No, nothing."

"I thought you were saying something. Aren't you going to give us a guided tour down Memory Lane?"

"That would be a bore for everyone. Here, August, we're just going through the gates of my family's estate."

"You sound like a realtor. Can't you just say 'house'?"

"I suppose I could. Now this is where the mansion itself stood, but the developers must have leveled it."

"Good riddance," Ernestine said. "Yellow stucco, wasn't it? Chocolate-brown trim?"

"It was a very gracious house—large sunny rooms and a grand piano."

"A *white* grand piano, if you can imagine. And concrete ledges beside the electric fire, ledges with brown foam rubber cushions. Aldwych, darling, you can hardly say the rooms were large and sunny. I remember them as painted yellow with a high gloss and stubbly surface. Ruthless overhead lights. All the furniture was spavined."

"Have it your way. As you can see the grounds were meticulously landscaped."

"Now, I suppose," Ernestine offered, "everything will be torn up to wedge in another McMansion. A gated community, everyone in golf carts, a high-tech kitchen next to a great hall with a cathedral ceiling and outsize Chinese vases from a decorator's storeroom, and a flowing carpeted staircase."

"Ernestine!"

"You know how it will look. An indoor lap pool a yard wide, twelve feet long, and stinking of chlorine under a whole battery of LED lights."

"This little house," Aldwych said, "was a double garage with the servants' quarters above."

"Remember, Aldwych, how your mother would tromp feverishly on the electric bell under the carpet?"

"No, I don't remember that."

"It was to summon Blanche, that poor old maid, to come clear the dinner plates and bring in the dessert. We used to laugh hysterically when your mother would get red in the face because Blanche had taken her hearing aids out."

"My mother was never cross. She was always gracious and charming to everyone."

"She could be pretty rude to your old lesbian wife. Now let's go and look at my father's house. I promise you it's not a building site. Bryce is restoring it to its 1920s grandeur. It's only ten minutes away."

14

August was audibly admiring of Ernestine's father's house and grounds, its many fountains and outbuildings and gazebos and its nut alley and greenhouses and potting sheds, its herbaceous borders, its screen of bamboo trees disguising the pump and generator. Ernestine seemed equally enthusiastic about the improvements Bryce had made—a vast columbarium; a baroque amphitheater all shells, water-slithery nymphs, and bearded tritons pulling the maidens onto their visibly excited laps; the *veuverie* and an exact copy of the queen's *laiterie* at Rambouillet down to the porcelain milk buckets painted to look like wood and the jugs of milk kept in a cooling stream. "This is paradise!" August exclaimed as he walked through the grounds past the hundred-year-old oaks.

As they were sauntering back to the car, Ernestine said, "Aldwych, you may be relieved to hear that I've found

August and me an apartment in a high-rise just a hundred paces from Lincoln Center. Yes, next to the Mormons—on the eighteenth floor. You'll be free to move darling Pablo into where August was staying."

"Pablo? Why Pablo?"

"We know," Ernestine said complacently, "that you two are a happy couple now. Congratulations! Pablo is quite the catch—handsome, affectionate, loyal, ardent."

"August is the only man in my life. What does Bryce think of your new . . . roommate?"

"He just wants me to be happy. And our new place will be so convenient to Lincoln Center. August can come back between class and rehearsal and get a . . ." (she wrinkled her nose in a kittenish way) "massage."

When they were alone, Aldwych asked, "Are you really going to live with her?"

"Does that upset you?"

"Why would it?"

"I guess I just float around in life and do whatever other people want."

"No, you don't. You do exactly what you want to do."

August didn't respond but picked at his cuticle.

"Do you know what that woman's all about?"

August looked up with his big gray eyes and shrugged.

"She's a sadist," Aldwych said vehemently.

"She warned me you'd try to undermine our relationship."

"August, I mean a real sadist. Not figuratively. She's abused my nephew Bryce. She's driven him crazy. You should have heard him going on and on the other day about the neglected heterosexual male's asshole."

"You're lying. You're lying. She's not like that. I love her!"

Aldwych had never seen August so red in the face, so vehement. After a moment, stunned, Aldwych said, "You do? You love her? I thought you were gay."

August literally wrung his hands and his voice was out of control. "She's saved me."

"From what?"

"From being queer. I never was queer. Not really. I was just screwed up by that Catholic Church. I thought lusting after a woman was a sin."

"It's not sinful. Just in poor taste, given the horrors of the patriarchy and overpopulation."

"It's not funny. If you knew how much I suffered. I always wanted a woman of my own, a beautiful dancer to whom I could be utterly devoted. I suffered so much from my little black teeth. And from my substandard French. And from my fear of women."

"Fear?"

"Yes, I was afraid. I was afraid I was inadequate. Impotent."

"Maybe you were just gay."

"I'm sure half the so-called gay men are like me. Afraid of not getting it up. I tried with girls, but they just lay there, white and fishy and quick to judge."

"Exactly. That's the problem with women."

"Not Ernestine! We clicked right away."

"With a little help from Pablo, right? He told me he had a finger or two up your ass."

"Don't be disgusting. You like to dirty everything sacred."

"I'm sure Ernestine herself would laugh to hear you call her sacred."

"Not her. But what we have."

"What do you have, in reality? A scrawny, horny post-menopausal woman and a lovely insecure boy whose ass is worshipped by every balletomane in New York."

"Why must you spoil everything? Ernestine is beautiful and pure. Our love is very pure. She's saved me from the self-hatred of being a pansy. Most gay men have had a few unfortunate encounters with harsh, mocking women who've sapped their self-confidence. They'd all prefer to be real men."

"You don't think I'm real? Or that Pablo is real?"

"Pablo will fuck anything that moves and count the legs later. He's just a phallus on wheels."

"Is that what I am?"

"You had an unfortunate marriage with a masculine lesbian."

"Is that Ernestine's theory?"

"No, it's what you told me. I don't think anyone's really gay. People want to feel proud, not despised. They want children. They want lifelong marriages. Men want to feel strong and muscular, protective and trustworthy. Some men are slimeballs, okay. Most gays are sweet, vulnerable men who've just taken the easy way out. They couldn't get it up, felt ashamed, and now they're all bottoms because that way they don't have to make an effort or prove anything. They can be boys forever, they can reject being dependable, responsible, they don't have to prove themselves since they're not supposed to do anything but suck cock and take it up the ass. They have to be beautiful as women, they have to have strong, muscular asses, but soon their holes start to sag and get too big, sloppy, roomy. They're not really desirable at thirty, less so at thirty-five, it's curtains at forty, whereas a straight man hits his peak at fifty, he becomes more and more worldly, he knows his wines . . ."

"Wines? What world are you living in? What century? And I haven't seen forty in decades—does that mean I'm washed up? Where did you get all these simplistic views of straight life?"

"I've just seen a few James Bond movies."

"And you're basing your vision of straight life on James Bond?"

. . .

The next day Aldwych phoned Bryce. "What's going on with your wife? She's scheming to take my August away from me."

"She warned me that you'd try to come between us."

"She's moving in with August in a one-bedroom on the West Side—don't you find something alarming in every detail of that sentence?"

"A lot of academics, perfectly respectable people, live on the West Side."

"August is twenty years old. Your wife is what? In her sixties?"

"You're in your seventies. Or more, right?"

"Aren't you jealous?"

"She's explained that I'm a physical wreck, utterly unworthy of her."

"Is that what she's explained. I'd say you're a good match."

"Don't be ridiculous. With my tummy and sagging tits and laughable little dick."

"So, she's apparently mocked you out of existence. I hate to think what she'll do to August."

"She worships him. His body. His passion. His flawless smile."

"Thanks to me he has a beautiful smile."

"You're a classic narcissist. Always inserting yourself into the story."

"She's leaving you and she's stealing my . . . my August!"

"He told her that you've never had sex together."

"He told her that?"

"Well, is it true?"

"If I were you I'd try to save my marriage, not probe into the intimate life of other people. You always were a snoop and a gossip, Bryce. Guess that comes from having no real life of your own."

"Yeah, you're right. I guess I am pretty pathetic. I think it would be fun to be cucked."

"What are you talking about?"

"Cucked. Cuckolded. That's a whole thing now—men tied up and forced to watch another man fuck their wives."

"That's disgusting, Bryce."

Bryce chuckled. "I guess I am pretty disgusting." He sounded highly satisfied.

"And I assure you," Aldwych said, "it's not a whole thing now, cucking, but only in your sick imagination." He sighed. "And it's pointless reproaching you. You just grab every insult and embrace it."

"Yeah, I am a worthless piece of shit."

. . .

That evening, when Pablo came into Aldwych's bed smelling of beer, Aldwych was sitting up reading *Nothing* by Henry Green and listening to New York's classical music station, though they were giving out prizes to mediocre student performers and inviting them to chat too much in their flat Midwestern accents. "Hey, Aldwych," Pablo said. "Whassup?"

"Nothing much. Just reading a book I read every year."

"Really?" He grabbed it and looked at it suspiciously. He sampled a few pages. "Why would you reread this?"

"It's funny."

"Oh, a joke book. I had one of those next to the crapper." He looked searchingly at Aldwych and kissed him. Aldwych thought he was a misplaced romantic, always talking about vile bodily processes while trying to smooch or wedging a rough thumb up Aldwych's anus and making doe eyes.

. . .

Mrs. Rothkopf, the German cook, was sharing a homemade lemonade with Rosita, the Panamanian housekeeper.

"I'm worried about Señor West. He don't look happy."

"It's true," Mrs. Rothkopf said. "He barely touches his food. Last night I made him a lovely schnitzel and he didn't eat a single bite."

"And he never forgets my birthday—yam a Libra— but this year he forget. And he traded in that nice Mr. Dupond—such an hidalgo—for that no-count Pablo."

"What's wrong with Pablo? He is very strong."

Mrs. Rothkopf poured her some more lemonade, then slapped fruitlessly at an autumn fly. "Why do you think Monsieur Dupond is moving out?"

"I think he's fallen in love with that witch Ernestine."

"But she's so old."

"*So* old." They didn't mention she was also female.

"Roger told me that she was very rude about Mr. West's family estate."

"She is very rude. Her husband is very nice, if a little eccentric. He's Mr. West's nephew. She's related only by marriage."

"The Wests are a very nice old family. I suppose you will be washing and ironing all Mister Pablo's clothes."

"Yes," Rosita said wearily. "Can you keep a secret?"

"Yes."

"When Mr. Dupond slept in Mr. West's bed there was never any mess. They could have been father and son. But now that that Pablo is sleeping there, there are often streaks of Mister West's doo-doo. Yellow. I recognize it from scrubbing the toilets. I have to change the sheets three times a week. Extra work. Do you think Mister West really forgot my birthday? Or is he having money problems?"

"I don't like serving good food to that rude *jüngling*—he never says '*Guten abend, Frau Rothkopf.*' And did you notice after he's cleared his plate he starts nibbling off Herr West's?"

Mrs. Rothkopf presented her theory that only rich people were genuinely homosexual—"They believe in small families, for inheritance reasons. The poor sleep with rich men just in order to get favors—do you say *favors?*"

Rosita wasn't sure what the right word was in English.

. . .

Ernestine's driver came with her to Aldwych's apartment to fetch August's few belongings. She slipped August two twenty-dollar bills and said, "Give one to Rosita and one to Frau Rothkopf. Tips. Rothkopf means 'redhead.' Do you think she ever had red hair? Of course those German women in advertising or publishing are always dyeing their hair red and wearing black leather. Black leather—someone called it the bad breath of fashion." Ernestine left desolation in her path.

Pablo moved in with some of his wrestling trophies. He was always getting in bed with Aldwych, spooning with him and falling noisily asleep. Aldwych knew he was ungrateful and irrational but he longed to be left alone to daydream about August. Nor did he like being buggered in the middle of the night, though he was in raptures before he was totally awake. Only when he realized where he was and with whom (not August in an idealized Mykonos) did he become resentful. He thought that Pablo smelled of olives and scorched red peppers, an odor as repulsive as his own grainy mustard-colored shit. Sometimes Pablo cleaned him up with a warm washcloth, but more often he let them sleep in his shit.

Pablo didn't have much conversation, though he was taking a course in acupuncture and talked a lot about *qi*. Aldwych had had wands stuck in him several times, which didn't do anything for him. He thought it was completely bogus. His acupuncturist had inserted his sticks and then gone into the next room to talk and laugh with another puncture operative. After forty minutes and a long conversation about Lady Gaga he'd finally come back and pulled the wands out. Aldwych had never been so bored.

15

Aldwych was sitting in the audience when August leapt very high in *Le Spectre de la Rose.* He was all pink tights, foliage-green arms, and a rose cap, a not very becoming bud that squeezed his features together. The girl, just back from the ball, was in a frothy dark blue evening gown, asleep in an armchair, theoretically dreaming of the souvenir rose. The music was Carl Maria von Weber, which Aldwych thought too stodgy for the action. He would have preferred a Franck cello sonata or something swoonier like that.

August looked a little thinner; Aldwych was sure that he was so besotted with Ernestine that he was staying up late with her. She was probably so proud of her new cavalier servente that she was dragging him along to all her pointless social engagements. The poor boy couldn't sleep alone and Ernestine was a night owl, watching old Doris

Day–Rock Hudson movies in bed, drinking old brandy and eating Turkish Delight or pistachios. She, who'd actually known Doris Day, pretended she was only now discovering Day's antique rom-coms ("I love them for their innocence"). Aldwych thought bitterly how she was teaching the boy all about American pop culture of the past, whereas he was a great artist, a noble steed, who should be fed only the rarest flowers of high culture— Mario del Monaco singing *Andrea Chénier*, Martha Graham dancing *Phaedra*, Helen Traubel and Groucho Marx in Gilbert and Sullivan. Aldwych scorned Ernestine's plebeian taste, which made her guffaw through *Schitt's Creek*.

But the worst of it was how exhausted August looked despite all the slaps on his face.

And then, as the Debutante dozed in her high-backed chair, the Rose leapt very high and landed with the loud snap of an unmoored muscle. He crouched in agony and hobbled offstage, bent over like an old man. Those members of the audience who were real balletomanes or retired dancers gasped and stood in alarm. The others, imagining that the accident was part of the choreography, smiled and looked around at the strange disturbance. The orchestra gradually subsided, *Titanic*-like, the curtain closed as the Debutante exited *en pointe* to the wings, the house lights came up, and everyone got up and tottered out into the mammoth lobby for some more bad champagne.

Aldwych collided with Ernestine at the stage door.

She: I hope it's not too serious.

He: Of course it's serious. He may never dance again.

She: (smiling) Seriously?

He: Yes, I'm serious, but I'm not sure you are.

She: Well, he can't dance forever. He's already twenty-five.

He: He could have danced another decade.

She: Now he won't have to. (pause) What do you think happened?

He: Late nights with you. Too much booze.

She: (outraged) Surely you're not blaming me.

He: He's a grown-up and can protect his own career, I suppose. (Cooling down) Zaza once told Mrs. Phipps they made him jump too high too young and his bones weren't ready for the shock.

She: What do you think happened? Oh, here's Zaza.

Zaza: Let me go. He needs me. A friend. A dancer.

He: We're friends too.

Zaza: Some friends aren't a good influence. A dancer's life is like a monk's life.

She pushed past them and hurried into August's dressing room.

The company doctor was crouched beside a seated August, whose face was turned to the wall. He looked around with an agonized grimace.

Zaza: Oh God, my baby, are you in horrible pain?

Doctor: I'm giving him injections for the pain.

Zaza: What happened to him?

Doctor: We'll know tomorrow. I've called an ambulance from New York Presbyterian. They have some of
the best orthopedic surgeons. It looks as if the Achilles
tendon snapped off his heel and has traveled all the way
up his calf. That usually happens to dancers and athletes
in their thirties. But an examination with the proper
instruments will show us. The main thing is to get him
out of pain and asleep.

Zaza: He has a *Prodigal Son* matinee tomorrow.

Doctor: That will make some lucky understudy's day.

Zaza: Will he ever dance again?

Doctor: Let's just say the Denver ballet is looking for
a director. But we'll operate and suture the break. He'll
probably wear a cast for six months—then he'll walk with
a little limp.

Although the doctor was whispering, August must
have heard something, for he started to cry.

As the gurney arrived with two nurses Aldwych and
Ernestine burst in.

Doctor: (to Zaza) Are these the parents?

Ernestine: (to the doctor) Lover. The lover.

The word was so lavish in the gray dressing room
it was like the sighting of an ermine in Akron. Aldwych
was outraged by her usurpation of that word and silently
swore vengeance.

"My angel, my sweet angel," Ernestine said, smothering August in kisses while the nurse pushed her away.

"Yes," Aldwych said, "we're the lovers, doctor."

August yelped, whether in pain or avid disagreement.

The doctor looked at Zaza and raised an eyebrow. "I didn't realize our patient was a gerontophile." He grabbed August's calf to see if his toes would bend downward (a sign the tendon was just bruised). The toes didn't bend, the ankle didn't flex—the tendon was severed.

Ernestine literally ground her teeth in rage, a sound no one had ever heard before or could readily identify.

Aldwych politely asked the ladies to a quiet dinner, but they each wanted to be alone. Truth be told, Aldwych wanted to be alone too. When Pablo staggered sleepily into his room, all furry flanks and half erect, Aldwych told him that he wasn't feeling well and wanted to sleep alone. Pablo sat on the edge of the bed for the longest time, massaging Aldwych's back, which was the last thing in the world he wanted. Aldwych lay there rigid with irritation until Pablo, now fully erect, slunk back to his room.

. . .

August was in the hospital for three weeks and then was sent by ambulance to a convalescent center where he would learn to walk again. He said to Zaza, "I looked at an old man today walking normally and I envied him so much. He could walk! I could just sit on the edge of this big black plastic surface on a low box; I'd pulled myself onto it by holding the attendant's hands. Day by day I see my legs lose muscle and bulk. One day I looked over my shoulder and saw that my ass, which had always been prominent but all muscle, was now just a sad little deflated thing. I guess without thinking about it I'd always been proud of my ass, especially when I wore white tights; I knew that all eyes, male and female, were trained on my big muscular butt. Half of the audience didn't know what they'd do with such an ass, but the other half knew perfectly well."

Zaza told him that he would regain his strength and form and go on to years and years of dancing, but they both knew it wasn't true. "You're in rehab. That's what rehab is for."

"It's just so terrible to see my muscles melting away."

He was placed in a chair and painless electric shocks were administered to his legs; the idea was that the shocks would awaken nerve growth or something. August was ready for a miracle cure. He was put in braces and encouraged to take a few terrifying steps. The trainer was harsh, but not as harsh as a ballet master. "You can do it!" Still in braces, August was ordered to ascend ten stairs and come down again. When he started to fall, the trainer caught him. The next day he was, braceless, supposed to get into a car—not a real car, but a plywood cutout the size of a car with a door on the side that slammed shut. Getting in and out of a car was seen as a major achievement and he was praised as he'd never been for his *sauts de Basque en manège*, the spectacular cart-wheels at the end of *Le Corsaire*.

When Aldwych came, August was asleep, but he woke at the sound of Aldwych noisily slipping out of his crinkly raincoat.

Aldwych: Oh, I'm sorry to wake you. You looked so peaceful.

August: Tranquilizers. Or pain pills.

Aldwych: Are you in a lot of pain?

August: Yes. Constant. But I'll survive.

Aldwych: (trying to sound casual) Have they said anything about your . . . prognosis?

August: (relentless) I may be able to walk again.

Aldwych: That's a blessing, I guess.

August: I guess.

Aldwych: I suppose I must call off Dietrich.

August: It's too late for that. You've already put down a deposit on the theater and advanced them a two-week security.

Aldwych: Surely they won't—

August: Do you have a special clause saying that if your boyfriend gets injured . . . ?

Aldwych: Of course not. But surely they must make exceptions, surely they must have some human feeling . . .

August: It's a *business*, Aldwych.

Aldwych: Don't sit up. I'm sorry I overexcited you. (Pause) How are you feeling? I mean, mentally.

August: Let's not go there.

Aldwych: Of course not. We'll have plenty of time to think about that.

August: Plenty of time . . . That's just what I'm afraid of.

Half an hour later August was falling asleep when Ernestine stepped into his room and August greeted her with an unaccustomed smile and shout of delight. "I recognized your perfume, Joy, before I could see you."

"My darling," Ernestine said. Glancing at Aldwych coldly, she said, "Oh, I hope you haven't been plagued by visitors. Not everyone learned from their mother that if you pay a call it should never last more than fifteen minutes."

"How would your mother know?" Aldwych asked. "She worked as a clerk at a fruit and vegetable store."

"That was just a summer job."

"A summer that lasted a decade until she hooked your father."

"Must you always talk such rubbish? And won't you give August and me some alone time?"

· · ·

After Aldwych's resentful departure, Ernestine sat beside August in bed and touched his erection through the top sheet. "Our big friend," she whispered. Then she moved to the visitor's chair and said, "I must try to behave."

"Why?" August asked. "If you only knew how happy you make me."

"Has the world ever seen such perfectly equal love?"

"Never. You've lifted this terrible curse of being gay off my shoulders."

"I doubt if you ever were really gay—in fact you've proved to me you're straight. Bigly." But she was thinking how everyone assumed all male dancers were gay and how August had stopped dancing the minute he became heterosexual.

She was secretly glad that August would no longer have to tour and practice and perform. She told him that she was buying them an A-frame beside a lake and that no one from their past would know where it was, certainly not Aldwych, that there they could begin their lives again as young lovers, far from the world. Her maid, Maria, who was Rosita's sister, she was letting go so that she wouldn't go back and tell Aldwych where they lived. No one would know—except darling Zaza of course, but she could be trusted. Ernestine showed him a realtor's photo of the A-frame—it looked rather lugubrious and far from the water for a man on crutches. But August pretended to be delighted by the prospect of solitude and straight sex around the clock. No more tedious classes, no more heart-stopping *tours en l'airs*, no more vomited dinners, no more fear of piss-spotting his white tights. No more grudging reviews. No more catty remarks behind the curtain as he took his bows ("Did you see how he can only turn to the right? And he's too short to partner anyone but Zaza. And he hasn't quite learned that second variation—he just stood still and looked confused during bars twelve through sixteen.")

When he got out of rehab he could walk to the corner with the help of his Rollator. He was afraid another dancer would see him in his physical disgrace. That would be humiliating to him and depressing to the other dancer. Was this the inevitable decline every dancer faced? August knew teachers whose feet were so deformed they could scarcely toddle across the room, who could still *plié* but not take a step.

In his dreams he skipped through the surf.

16

A month later, August had relearned to go up and down stairs and to get in and out of a car, and sensation had come back to his right foot and calf. He was so sick of the hospital food he could scarcely finish it, and he'd lost weight, which as an athlete he took as a loss of being. The only thing that fanned him back into living and a glimpse of pleasure was Ernestine's love. The way she looked at him with aching devotion, her wonderful perfume, the way she touched his erection through the sheet—these were the only bright moments of his day.

The automatic shrieks his bed made if he tried to get out of it to piss humiliated him. The long, pained looks Aldwych cast at him left him feeling defeated and depressed. Even Zaza's cheerfulness and robust health felt like a reproach, as if he'd taken the wrong path at the fork and now he could only stare at her diminishing figure in the dying light. She became smaller and smaller, more and more distant. Ernestine was the only person beckoning him into a quiet, sexy future hidden from everyone else.

She had hired a driver and a limousine for his escape. The rules held that he must leave the convalescent center in a wheelchair manned by a nurse, but he stood when unbelted and slipped into the seat in the much-rehearsed fashion. In the last month the forsythia had started to blaze, and the privet hedge looked fuller and less dusty. The light descended in brilliant shards as if a window had been shattered. He had to hold his hand up as a visor. He'd forgotten the world. Cars were slithering like bright, colorful beetles down the street. Children were laughing and shoving each other. Pedestrians were crossing the street wherever they wanted. Everyone was shouting. Sunlight dazzled on high windows. The pretzels being sold by the vendor in his metal-clad cart smelled delicious.

It wasn't far to their Lincoln Center apartment, but August looked out greedily at each building, each pedestrian, each car that glided past. It was as if every familiar object had been dipped in glaze.

When he thought about what had happened to him, his accident had been so unforeseen, his recovery even less a given but slow, so gradual after the catastrophe of the snapped tendon that he could scarcely observe it, a glacial sag after the sudden avalanche. Of course he'd been operated on, and the anesthesia and then the morphine for the pain had obliterated a few days. Then the unreality of seeing a brilliant career evaporate in a second had left him confused—stunned. There hadn't even been any articles about it in the paper.

His every waking second had been obsessed with dance, with class and rehearsal and performance, with bleeding feet and pulled muscles, which he was always supposed to ignore and work through. What he ate, how he stretched, how he slept, even the ballet YouTubes he watched, the lore about Petipa and Fokine and Balanchine and Robbins and Tharp, the cocks he sat on—every moment had its consequences. Its advantages. Its damages.

That was all in the past now. Sometimes as he lay in bed, half asleep, he would imagine his way through his steps—his face turned to the ceiling to dramatize his elevation, his left arm sweeping in an arc across his chest to give himself momentum for his first turn, his elbows close to his body as he went into a rapid series of turns—oh, it was all pointless now. He couldn't even walk, or barely, a Frankenstein monster with a rickety, stumbling, perilous gait.

He liked the little meals that Ernestine prepared. He liked lifting her small breasts and feeling their light weight in his hands. He liked when she slid down to his waist and sucked him, but that confused him too because he'd always been the bottom, the one who sucked, who got fucked, who moaned with pleasure even when it hurt or bored him. Bottom because it was safer—what if he couldn't get hard? He knew his ass was superb, trained—or had been. By reflex he thought he should be doing something more, licking her nipples, fingering her twat, battering her asshole, sifting her hair to one side, nibbling her ear, which was always redolent of Joy. He felt hollowed out, absent, just submitting—but everything physical was strange and new to him now that he was a physical being without a body.

After he'd recovered for three days they went out to a café. August was self-conscious about his weight loss, and he noticed that few people looked at him. He was used to being heavily cruised by men and some women. Only three months ago he'd been standing on the corner waiting for Zaza when a well-dressed middle-aged woman had started talking to him. "I saw you looking around. Are you a tourist?"

"No, not at all, just waiting for a friend."

She'd moved closer and said confidentially, "I'm very good at fellatio."

August laughed and said, "So is my boyfriend."

She shrugged and walked on. She didn't seem that amused.

He was worried that another dancer might see him, and he wished his Rollator wasn't so large. Then he kept checking out young men with prominent asses in tight, worn jeans and reproached himself for cruising males, if that was what he was doing. Now that he was an invalid (he paused over *not-valid*) he looked at muscular hotties with the same confusion he'd always felt. Did he want to have them or be them? Did he admire them or envy them? Did he want to submit to them or dominate them? Probably submit. As he looked at those big muscular asses, he could taste them—salty, rancid, hot. Chthonic. He felt guilty toward Ernestine, who was sitting right there, looking radiant and unsuspecting.

Would he never be completely cured? When he was alone with Ernestine he thought only of her, and when he penetrated her he felt he was the only man on earth and a glorious, perfect example of one, even with his infirmities. But now, in public, looking at those muscular asses, he felt feeble, faithless, seduced: traitorous. How could he betray his poor Ernestine like this? Alone with his Eve he was Adam; surrounded by other men he was no one.

. . .

Aldwych lost all interest in ballet now that August no longer danced. He let the more and more frequent letters and emails from Dietrich accumulate; if he thought of it, he forwarded them to his lawyer, Laurence Butter-field, who sent him a message marked "Urgent," which he opened.

"Dear Aldwych, you have signed on to debts with M. Dietrich which, if they're not earned out, will vacate your entire fortune, your apartment and limousine included. All that will remain is a cottage in Saugatuck, Michigan, which, following my counsel, we did not integrate into your estate. Your father's maiden aunt Sandy (a lesbian surely—it's a notorious gay community) left it to you in her will. Look it up on the map—you may be living there. Fatefully, L.B. We must talk."

. . .

Aldwych wondered what life would be like as a poor man. Thankfully he wouldn't have to live much longer, humiliated by poverty as he would be. His attention darted among his friends and few remaining relatives, asking himself which of them if any would take him in. Would he move to Saugatuck and find the love of his life? They had an artists' colony there, he'd heard. Would there be any sweet gerontophiles there?

His usual tactic was to make a substantial contribution to any artists' group that interested him and then wait to meet the gleeful organizers, but now it seemed he'd be poor and unable to ingratiate himself. An unattractive old man with tomb hairs in his ears and nose, *une petite nature,* penniless and friendless, deprived by a life of privilege of any cunning or even worldliness, gifted with beautiful manners that wouldn't be noticed in someone so poor he had to be polite—this was the new order he was being initiated into.

He wanted to see August. Aldwych had cleared out every last vestige of the boy's residence in his apartment.

Nothing remained as traces of his long stay. Where was he? He hated Ernestine for kidnapping the boy and keeping his whereabouts secret. He knew their apartment was near Lincoln Center. Should he canvass all the buildings in the neighborhood? No, Ernestine would be too wily to display her name on the building's call buttons. He realized they had no mutual friends except Pablo, who didn't know where they were, and her wretched husband Bryce, who might pretend he was "afraid" she would flog him if he confided their address. Hadn't she said it was on the eighteenth floor, near the Mormons?

He ached with love for August, especially late at night. Every morning he could hope that August would get in touch with him and email, "I made a terrible mistake. Now I know I love you, that we were destined for each other. Please take me back, I beg of you. I haven't been able to sleep a full night since I left you."

As each day wore on, Aldwych realized no such message would be coming—he knew August went to bed early, that he was too proud ever to write an email like that, that in any event he was besotted with Ernestine and that she, who'd always been considered ugly, treasured the love of this young matinee idol. And the boy had no money and Ernestine had lots.

Aldwych wondered again whether he'd really lose everything and have to live in Saugatuck. Would he meet people? He wouldn't have any staff—could he entertain? What if he had a stroke and couldn't drive? Or didn't own a car? He hoped Ernestine would have the stroke, but she was too skinny and tough to have one. *A tough old bird,* he thought.

He'd never quarreled with August or touched him "inappropriately," as people said now. It was an outrage that he didn't know where they were living. Both August and Ernestine had blocked him on their phones and Ernestine had fiddled with her Skype. All too despair-making, as his late mother would put it (she'd lived in Bristol as a teen and ridden with the Wilts Hunt on the Duke of Somerset's estate, where the dogs were of a breed from the 1600s).

· · ·

One afternoon August ran into another young male dancer, who always wore makeup and trousers tight in the rear. August was limping his way through a glass revolving door when he saw Kyle, who revolved around a full circle and hugged him. "Oh, doll, I heard what happened, you poor angel." They talked for a while; August was ashamed of his limp and his dramatic weight loss. "Darling," Kyle said, "wherever are you living? Even poor Aldwych didn't seem to know when I called the house." He fluttered his eyelashes and asked in a camp bass whisper, "And with *whom*?"

"I will never dance again, but I've found the love of my life."

"You hussy! Who is he?"

"It's actually a she."

"A she? A she? And what do you do—bump pussies?"

"I love her. She's an extraordinary woman."

"I never look at women. Ugh! I don't like women."

"They're not a category." August smiled. "They're individuals. As different one from one another as men are."

"You couldn't prove it by me. I never look at them. And they smell like old tuna left to rot in the sun."

"Well, nice seeing you."

"Wait! I didn't mean it. Just the bitch in me talking." Kyle took his hand. "I'm happy for you. Genuinely happy." He said *genuine* to rhyme with *wine* and smiled and opened his eyes as wide as they'd go. "Whatever makes you happy. After all that's gone down. I just never would have guessed you had those *tendencies*." He glanced at his wrist. "My Lady Bulova says I must skedaddle. So good to see your *eek*—that's Polari for 'face.'" They exchanged two air kisses, one on each cheek.

That little encounter left August profoundly depressed. Was he just kidding himself about his conversion to heterosexuality? He tried to train himself not to look at men's crotches—it was just a nasty habit, but could he break himself of it? When straight guys would say, "You know who I mean—the top-heavy chick," he realized he didn't know, he didn't usually check tits out, not as he did big meat swelling under Levi's buttons or filling out the pleat going down the left leg ("He dresses left" was a phrase that could undo him). Did he like women or just one magical woman?

Now that he was broken, he longed to be abused by a man or maybe just fucked hard. He wanted to be treasured for his flaws, his inadequacies—wasn't that the whole idea of masochism? Isn't that why slaves like to be insulted?

In the past when he'd been feverish, or when his muscles ached or his throat was sore, he'd been submerged by waves of wanting to submit to a perfect, healthy young man: with the emblem of a double-headed eagle woven in hair on his powerful chest; with pubic hair nearly brown in contrast to the blond hair on his head; with the hair on his butt thickening and turning black as it approached his crack (at once inviting and forbidding); with the artery climbing asymmetrically toward the dome of the rock, red and shaped like an upside-down exclamation mark.

Oh, it was all too silly and overwhelming, this desire to submit, these flights of bad poetry before the tools of a reluctant torturer, for didn't most gay men want to get fucked, and today's trade is tomorrow's competition? Don't most tops long to bottom? Wouldn't your master leave you to become another man's slave?

Ernestine and he got stoned that evening and had good sex. They got the munchies and ordered in mac and cheese and bacon. She noticed he was in a mood and asked him what was wrong. He turned his pillow over to the cool side, sat up, sucked air, and said, "I'm afraid I'm not right for you. I can't stop thinking about men. You deserve someone who's a hundred percent straight."

She said, "That would bore me terribly. Straight men are overconfident. Gay men are too self-doubting. You're just right."

"Like the baby bear's bed? But I keep fantasizing about guys."

"Do you think you can stay faithful to me?"

"Of course I can. You're my life. You're my reason for living." He looked down at his hands, quiet and cupped as though he were holding something. "I've never been in love before." He said it as if embarrassed or ashamed.

She said, "You're the great love of my life."

He looked at her through tears. "Really?"

She kissed him, stared into his eyes, and said, "Really."

Their food arrived. It was still warm and cheesy and she found two bits of clear plastic in her macaroni but didn't complain or even mention it. With Bryce she'd have made a terrifying fuss. She'd brought out good china and silver and damask napkins, then a bottle of cold Chinon rosé and two stemmed glasses. They watched a silly show on TV about rap singers staging a comeback, then August fell asleep, though it was only nine thirty. She turned off the television. For hours she sat vigil in the dark gazing at her golden boy.

In the morning she always woke up half an hour before August and brushed her teeth and hair, dabbed herself with Joy, changed into a fresh nightgown. She studied herself in the mirror, not harshly but realistically, as an older woman will do, before climbing back into bed and pretending to sleep.

Later, after they'd both had coffee and toast with smoked salmon and were sitting in the kitchen at their round imitation fifties breakfast table with the aluminum band around the circumference, she smiled and took his hand and placed it on her left breast.

She said, "When you fantasize about men, what do you think about?"

"Being dominated."

Oh, no, she thought—*another* one—but she smiled and said, "That's because you're injured. Everyone who's injured feels vulnerable."

He looked at her with huge eyes full of surprise and trust. "Really? Is that right?" He wanted to believe her. She had just absolved him.

"Right as rain."

She tucked away the news that he was a masochist. She had no need to unfurl the black cape of domination over him, not just yet. He was so visibly in love with her that her words and smiles controlled him absolutely. But if ever his ardor dimmed she knew now how to revive it; she'd contrive to look as if she was discovering the giving and taking of pain at the same moment he was.

It gave her a thrilling sense of peace to know she had endless resources with this young man. Now August truly belonged to her, as a swain for the moment and a slave for the future.

She drove August out to look at the house on the lake. The A-frame was freckled darker where the rain had splattered the wood. It had huge windows. Even from the outside the interior looked a mess.

The front door had two purple windows high up. At last Ernestine found the key and opened the door. They were hit with a sour odor as if there was a leak somewhere and the carpet was mildewing in one room. "Oh, I shouldn't have brought you out until I'd cleared all the McTeers' crap out. You're going to have such a bad impression. Men never have vision."

August assured her that he did have "vision" and could see this was going to be their perfect love nest.

He wondered what kind of life the McTeers must have led. In what must have been the "master" bedroom there were angled floor-to-ceiling mirrors and a big flat mirror on the ceiling above the bed. In the bedside table there was a Spanish grammar and a hair dryer that didn't work. The bedspread for the queen-size bed was of some sleazy synthetic, printed with big dahlias and burned on one corner by the pie-slice of an iron. There were paper sunflowers in a yard-high blue vase of glass with bubbles in the glass, the bubbles too regularly spaced to be a glassblower's mistakes. "Very Pier One," Ernestine said dismissively of a chain of bargain stores. August thought he might have heard of it.

As they explored the ugly house with its cheap left-over furnishings and its evil smells (the kitchen was truly foul), August was becoming more and more depressed. So much sordid dailiness weighed on him. His mother's house was just as impoverished, but the benches and tables had been carved by human hands out of trees felled in their yard. Here everything was a tacky machine-made version of itself, more often Formica or particle board than cloth or brass or real wood with heft and traces of its fashioning. There were hundreds of discarded magazines and Sunday supplements in a broken wooden cradle. In the cupboards (the exteriors painted a chipped green, the interiors still raw wood) they found a fondue set, outsize plastic forks from some missing salad bowl, a chipped mug from an Ohio motel.

The McTeers favored the ersatz over the real—or maybe they thought junk was good enough for their second house and their summer renters. Ernestine imagined they were the kind of people who kept a detailed inventory for renters of all these horrors—she hadn't met them.

The toilets in the airless bathrooms had bowls stained tan at the water level and poisonous "air fresheners" hanging from the towel cupboard. In the TV room there was a weird-shaped couch along one wall; the fabric was blanketed with dog hair (blond and white—a collie, no doubt). The TV was still there; the only thing that played was the DVD—they looked at a home movie of a grandmother in black hobbling about, laughing point-lessly, toothless and speaking Spanish while embracing dirty children.

After this heartrending tour, Ernestine found a bit of paper and made a list. "First we hire workers to clear everything out, pull up the carpets, call the junkman, find a team to repaint everything, install a new kitchen and bathrooms, replant the grounds—we'll need a service to coordinate everything."

"That sounds expensive."

"It will mainly be time-consuming, but we should be able to move here in two months." She looked up. "Is that all right, my darling?" She put a breath freshener in her mouth and kissed him. She loved his plush lips and his big strong tongue when it came out of his mouth like a snail from its shell. His newly capped teeth were white as tiles. She examined his emaciated face and regretted the youthful glow he'd lost in just the last two months. He'd been kept in a coma with fentanyl for four days after his leg surgery. He'd lain there unconscious under a light blanket, his penis available to her whenever the nurse was away; she just needed to stand beside him to block the view of anyone coming through the door and make his penis hard and then move the bedding aside so she could look at it, this thing that with any luck would belong to her from now on, this talisman so many dance fans had surmised or intuited late at night in their lonely beds, this scepter that had ruled over so many bent heads, this ivory

Derringer that fitted into the hand so neatly, this plush-sheathed bar of steel that throbbed into glowing life at a touch: this destiny. Was she "kinky" for exploring him while he lay unconscious? But wasn't this the freedom lovers enjoyed with each other? Anyway no one would ever know, least of all August. She studied his slack, inert face; no sign of awareness.

. . .

Before they moved, August heard her on the phone haggling with vendors. Twice a week she'd drive out to the building site to supervise the work. Or rather she was driven by her driver. She had the crown in their lane lowered so that it wouldn't scrape the bottom of the low-slung car. The path was replanted to look like a country lane—the changes cost her $100,000. Two months later they'd moved into what Ernestine called their "cottage." It was so completely transformed that August could scarcely believe it was the same place. Even the surrounding trees looked different, already sprouting new leaves. The ground was less muddy; somehow Ernestine had conjured rolling lawns and purple crocuses. Inside, everything was spare and spacious. The horrible posters the McTeers had fancied were banished; there was just one large signed Ansel Adams photo, of mountains. Ernestine had to explain to him who Adams was.

The walls were iceberg white, the pleated curtains the color of sand and so thin you could see through them the trees outside and the distant lake. The kitchen was a miracle of clean lines with its big Aga stove and its walnut cupboards stocked with canned foods (even a big tin of duck confit, the brown and orange label in French). Elsewhere there were plain green gold-rimmed coffee cups and saucers you could find in a Paris café.

All the mirrors had been removed from the bedroom. The matching round bedside tables were of split straw under glass; Ernestine confessed they were by Jean-Michel Frank, who'd made them in the 1920s. She'd bought them last week at Sotheby's for just $75,000—"a steal."

"Then I'll be extra careful with them," August said.

She stroked his cheek with the back of her hand.

He was secretly surprised the lighting wasn't recessed as at Aldwych's (wasn't that what rich people had?). Instead she had blue-and-white Chinese vases wired up as lamps with shades of stretched ecru silk. The bulbs were very low wattage—in fact they were unfrosted strangely bulbous Edison bulbs, he learned. So that they could read in bed there were hidden spotlights, each on its own dimmer.

The three bathrooms were fitted with big steampunk fixtures that the designer had excavated out of condemned Edwardian houses (there was a freelance studio on White Street that found and restored such things as well as carved marble fireplaces). The tub was of mottled brass set in a wooden frame; everything smelled deliciously of wood. The shower had five sprinklers at various heights and angles. There was also a small wood sauna. August tried not to exclaim too much; exclaiming might be one of the things that Ernestine found vulgar, or, as she would say in French, *"populaire."* She had already taught him not to laugh, just smile; friends interpreted no laughter as a sign of his underlying sadness or attributed it to his teeth, which they didn't know had been replaced.

In the first enthusiasm of their affair, Ernestine wanted to learn *joual* so that she could communicate with August's parents. He kept telling her that she should learn "real" French, but she argued that that revealed his colonial inferiority complex—"Your French is more savory and supple than what the French Academy has produced; it's like Yiddish as compared to German. It's rich with history and feeling."

In these disputes August felt in over his head. He'd been persuaded his *joual* was comical and no more than an unwritten patois; what did it mean beside Racine or Molière? He was touched that Ernestine wanted to learn French Canadian, however, and when they were in the car they agreed to speak only *joual*. The rule reduced Ernestine to silence, which she soon gave up for English.

For the first two months Ernestine was fascinated by August (whom she started calling "Auguste," in the French pronunciation)—to the point that she would draw him when he was asleep and even push him into different positions and spread his legs, which would often awaken him. She kept him nude most of the time when they were home. He sat in the kitchen while she was scrambling eggs and she sat in the little gym when he was working out. She offered to get him a trainer but he said to wait a month or two until he was stronger and would feel more confident about exposing his body. When he went to the toilet she said that she wanted to try something. While he sat and shat she knelt before him and gave him a blow job. He worried about the smell engulfing them. He remembered how it had felt in a three-way when one partner had fucked him and the other had sucked him. But he mainly thought what it would be like to be in her place, kneeling before an erect man, trying to take the whole thing, feeling his fingers twisting your nipples, his toes reaming your "cunt," his hand pushing your head farther and farther down on his dick, cumming, then presenting his shitty ass to your mouth and tongue to clean.

After he came, August stood, wiped his ass and said very softly, "That was so intimate." She pressed her tits together and licked her lips—very porn film, he thought. "I always wanted to try a blumpkin," she said, and laughed. He was appalled, not by doing it but that it had a name. That meant it was a common thing, that other people did it, that they could joke about it.

. . .

But then one day she began to shrug him off when he tried to embrace her. She said irritably, "Get off me. I'm reading!" and she waved the copy of *Vogue*, though in fact she was only peeling back the sample perfume strips and sniffing them.

He remembered how she'd said she was easily bored. Was he boring her? He didn't have any conversation except about ballet and his childhood in Canada and he'd discovered she knew nothing about dance and didn't care about it, and Canada was terminally boring for sophisticated New Yorkers. Most of them had been to Quebec once, and all agreed the food was good, though one smartass had said Quebec was Cleveland with substandard French and a few good restaurants. Gays liked the go-go boys who would fuck you for a few Canadian dollars.

He panicked. He thought how he didn't have any money or skills. Or any friends except Aldwych, who seemed to be with Pablo now. Maybe they'd take him in for a week while he looked for work. Did that mean he'd have to be gay again, laugh at their jokes, discuss penis size at the dinner table, watch *The Golden Girls* on TV, laugh at off-color innuendos, listen to Lana Del Rey, let guys grab his ass or crotch? Would his "affairlet" with a woman intrigue some gays who spoke of their rectums as their "cunts" or cause those who assumed it had been sexless, that he'd just been Ernestine's walker, to laugh at his low self-esteem? "You should see a therapist," he could already hear them saying. "I did and now I'm a proud bottom, though a year ago I was a confused self-hating

Baptist kid in Kansas pretending like you to want some pussy but only after marriage, please, preferably with a female ice hockey player, pity we had to adopt, guess I was just sterile . . . What a farce!"

He was silent most of the afternoon. "Shall I make dinner?" he asked.

"No, God, I'll put a bullet through my brains if I have to stay in again this evening."

"If you want to invite some friends out for a few days, that would be fine."

"And what? Talk about your surgery or your child-hood in the sticks? The way you tapped the maples for syrup? I'm sure they'd be fascinated."

He fought back the tears and said, "Maybe I should get a job, so you have some alone time."

"Doing what?"

"Waitering, maybe."

"You can hardly walk. Auggie, let's face it. You're a cripple. No one would hire you." She held up a page in *Vogue* for his inspection. "Do you think this is too young for me?"

"Not at all. But maybe get it in plum, your best color." He smiled. "These are the sort of clothes that my mother would say no woman would ever wear."

"I guess you never see them at the mall or church or the ball game, your mother's public events."

He smiled.

"If you were working, what would I do in this goddam wilderness? I suppose I could invite Bryce out. He says he misses me."

August felt a pang of jealousy. Would she sleep in Bryce's room or his?

He was afraid he'd say the wrong thing, so he went back to the weight room in the basement. He was working out hard each day, trying to get some bulk in his chest and arms, some strength in his withered legs and buttocks. If he was some sort of gigolo, he might as well be an appetizing one. It bothered him that he didn't have any money of his own except for the small check he'd get from Warburton once a month—the company's retainer fee. He wasn't sure what it was for, but he remembered they'd bargained hard for it and almost gone on strike.

As he lifted weights he felt better. He'd added five pounds on each side of the barbell this week and his biceps were really pumped. He lay on his stomach on a board and hooked a weighted pulley behind his calves. He scissored his legs up and could feel the strain in his buttocks and thighs. He was slowly rebuilding his body, though he knew he would never dance again.

If Ernestine asked him to leave, where could he go? He knew he could stay with Zaza for a while. He had a friend who owned a Lucite furniture store on the Upper East Side. Maybe he could work there—he would attract a few fans to the store, maybe even get some press. But he hated the idea of all those gays pretending to shop when they just wanted to meet him; he dreaded their noticing how he'd aged and lost his looks and mobility. Of course he could teach dance somewhere—in Idaho, say—but he dreaded small-town life after New York, dreaded working with young dancers who could do steps he could no longer manage.

After dinner at a cozy restaurant with a fireplace, low lights, and mediocre food (they each drank three Manhattans), and since after ten o'clock they were the only customers except an obese couple at the bar, they asked the waiter if it would be all right if they each smoked a cigarette, which he was persuaded to give them from his pack of Gauloises. "Don't make a habit of it," he said with a smile.

Back in the A-frame they got stoned. She told him to get undressed, which he did without comment or question, though she didn't make a move toward taking off her own clothes. She began to work his nipples, which hurt a bit but also excited him. She pulled his erection away from his body and it snapped back onto his stomach. She squeezed his balls, which hurt but made him even harder. Very deliberately she squeezed some lubricant on her right index finger and pushed it quickly into his ass—which made him yelp and caused a drop of precum to appear at the tip of his penis.

"Feel good?" she asked.

He bowed his head in silent assent.

"I want you to say it loud and clear."

"It feels good, mistress."

She dropped her voice, smiled and said, "I thought it might."

He was so pleased that he was back in her good or at least better graces, that he could still fascinate her, or at least his anus could. He wondered if other women and men played this way. Or was she perverted? Or was he?

Did she like him more or less?

Did his easy acquiescence in obeying her make him seem more or less a man in her eyes?

She had a way of talking about their relationship at a dinner party and saying more to strangers than she'd ever confide to him in private. Many New Yorkers were like that, floating a shocking revelation in public as if it were only meant to entertain. The more exalted their status, the more revelatory they were about even scurrilous things. The people who knew they were unassailable took the biggest risks. She had said at a dinner, "I like to be the man—not with lesbians but with sissy men or gay men or just men. I like to be the top."

That had made everyone laugh or gasp and look at poor Bryce. *So that explains it,* most of them must have thought. That's why she's with such a milquetoast, such a nebbish. His lack of balls isn't a problem; for her it's an advantage. People had surrendered to a queasy look, a sort of crooked smile. Was she being funny or truthful? Of course, as all stand-ups know, the comic begins with the painfully honest.

August had been at that dinner. He barely knew them then. Aldwych had invited him. That was at the very beginning, long before Pablo. August had made a mental note of that remark. He wasn't used to this sort of daring conversation. He'd hung out with a few cheeky dancers, like that Kyle who wore eyeliner. But most of them were serious professionals from the Midwest who spoke modestly. They were middle-class kids from Toledo who'd started ballet classes as little girls (the boys usually had taken a less obvious route, usually involving a sister or an older boyfriend). They were generally polite to the point of being colorless. They were competitive but seldom openly so. They were all "nice," exemplars of that kid-next-door suburban niceness that most youngsters could assume as protective coloring (the lizard who looks like a leaf unless it moves or climbs black bark). They chattered in the lingua franca of American banality that everyone spoke ("Wanna hang, dude?") though it expressed nothing and would soon sound as silly as the Beats, those "crazy cats."

Oddly enough, August had felt his penis stiffening at Ernestine's words. Her wild claim of wanting to dominate men excited him. He did sometimes have fantasies of being dominated, but they always vanished once he'd come; he'd acted on those fantasies only once and scarcely allowed himself to elaborate them in solitude (he always came quickly while masturbating). Once a guy he'd met on a sex site irritated him so much ("Don't touch my hair!") that he'd slapped him and the guy came in a second. They got together twice after that and August enjoyed, sort of, roughing him up.

The masochist told him about the Eagle, a bar for the S&M crowd, but August never had the courage to visit it. What if there were people there from the dance world? Fans?

He'd already confessed to Ernestine that he harbored thoughts of being dominated by men, which she'd excused as being an invalid's thought. But maybe, with her superior insight and richer experience, she'd divined that he wanted to be pushed around, barked at and hurt, by *n'importe qui*, man or woman.

She let Bryce come out once so that August and she could torture him. She knew how much Bryce would appreciate it, and it would open August's eyes to what she was capable of. Naturally Bryce had to be sworn to secrecy as to their whereabouts; they didn't want Aldwych dropping in, though Bryce was encouraged to tell Aldwych that he'd been topped by both of them. She liked the thought of building up her legend as a sadist and indicating that they were a dangerous couple, not bland as their lakeside A-frame might suggest. It was as if a stray cat taken in might turn out to be a killer—something demonic.

But Bryce turned up with their ailing aunt as if it were a family visit. "Why did you bring *her*?" Ernestine whispered loudly.

"Poor thing, she's not long for this world."

"If you'd come alone *you* could have been the poor thing. You could have served two masters."

"Two?"

"Wake up—August and me."

"Oh, I really goofed up, didn't I?"

"Not if you prefer being kind to older, failing aunts than to having your ass bloodied."

"Perhaps next weekend?"

"It's not a standing offer."

"Oh, dear."

"And what's this talk of weekends? It's not as if we have jobs. We're 'off' every day."

August made them all crustless chicken sandwiches with lots of mayonnaise, and blue Mariage Frères tea. Aunt Wilma was astonished by the blue tea.

"You're a very nice boy," she said, looking up at August through her pink-rimmed glasses with her slightly dotty expression. "Do we know each other? Are you a relative?"

"No, "August said. "I'm a friend of Ernestine's."

"Lucky Ernestine. Are you a male nurse?"

"Well, I am male. Not a nurse. I don't do anything."

"Join the crowd," Wilma said with a rueful smile. "Are you one of the Lille Duponds?"

"No, no. I'm a nobody."

"Join the crowd," Wilma said sweetly, though in her case it wasn't the truth.

When pressed, August finally admitted that he'd been a ballet dancer. "Oh," Wilma said, "I studied with a student of Martha Graham's. You're awfully young to have retired."

"I had an injury."

"How terrible."

She was too polite to ask for details.

When their visitors left, Ernestine said, "Bryce missed out on a memorable session."

"Wilma is sweet."

Ernestine said, "She's a frightful old bore."

Despite a light rain, they walked to the lake holding a flashlight.

17

In the middle of the night Aldwych woke up with a brainstorm. He would find out from Pablo where Ernestine and Auggie lived. He was probably sending checks every month to August and must have his address; August wouldn't forgo his salary, no matter how small.

Aldwych felt that killing them would be no great loss. Ernestine, that evil bitch, deserved to die. Anyway her life bored her; she wouldn't miss it. And no one would miss her. She hadn't befriended anyone in a deep way. She had no children. Bryce would miss her cruelty, but he'd find another dominatrix soon enough. Their servants would stay on with Bryce, who'd treat them better. Her father's house would be a memorial to both Ernestine and her father. He thought he should rewrite his will in favor of Bryce; that way he'd be contributing to their posthumous renown.

In a hundred years they'd all be forgotten, but poor people would go to their estate for a nice picnic and visitors would wonder who had lived there—if anyone on earth was still alive a hundred years from now.

As for August, he had nothing to live for. He'd never dance again, and that was the only thing he'd ever cared about. He could exult in his factitious heterosexuality but that would quickly become tiresome, being scrawny Ernestine's toyboy or, worse, her slave!

Should he kill August first so that Ernestine could mourn him a moment before her own death? He'd reread the murder scene in *Crime and Punishment* in which Raskolnikov cracks open the old moneylender's skull with an ax and then, when her feeble sister returns by surprise, axes her too.

Aldwych didn't think he would choose an ax—what if they grabbed it out of his hand? They were both stronger than he. Then what? Would they just all sit around on the floor, laughing at the farce they'd made of their lives and deaths? Or would they be really angry and ax him? Ernestine could do that. There'd be no witnesses out there in the snowbound A-frame. They could have a field day with him. Ernestine might want to torture him first—that would be just like her. August probably would put up a minor objection. He was kindhearted. Not an eye-for-eye kind of guy.

Aldwych guessed he'd choose a gun, easy to buy in America, really a patriotic choice. Constitutional. He'd be testing his rights while getting revenge. Maybe he'd shoot August in his bad leg and let him and Ernestine take it all in, that he was serious this time. Let August suffer a little, just as he'd made Aldwych suffer.

Of course, he'd warned Aldwych from the beginning not to fall in love with him.

Might as well warn the fox not to eat the chicken, or the child not to touch the blueberry pie.

Dietrich wrote asking what sort of press he'd organized for him. Aldwych didn't reply. He thought he'd shoot himself after he'd polished off the others. He couldn't think of himself as poor any more than he could think of himself as not male—they were "baked in," as they said on TV, his wealth and his gender, though neither amounted to much. Anyway, he didn't want a "creature of the underworld," as he thought of ballet people for no good reason, angry at him. French people, they said, could be especially cutting.

Laurence Butterfield called him early one morning (at ten) and said, "Hope you're ready for Michigan 'cuz it looks like Saugatuck for you."

"Why? What's happened?"

"You know how you asked the patrons of your ballet season to look at YouTubes of Dietrich's work?"

"Yes."

"They all did. And didn't like it. Too muscular and masculine for them. Not enough floaty white tutus. Anyway, they've all backed out of their pledges."

"They can't do that!"

"Yes they can. You didn't make them sign anything."

"I have their word of honor."

"Good luck on that."

. . .

When Aldwych looked back at his long life, he thought he'd suffered most over love, first with women, then with men. Women were a little kinder because they were more impressed by money than first-world men were. You had to move to the second world (Poland, Romania) before wealth gave you any traction. Best of all was the third world (Egypt, Morocco, Benin), where every man was available but you had nothing in common except your ass.

He'd never worked out. His dick was small. With gay men you had to be as successful as a man and as beautiful as a woman—not beautiful in a feminine way but extremely buff. Nor did American men admire the merely rich. You had to be a professional—doctor, lawyer, engineer, even dentist. Just wearing beautiful clothes and living at a chic address wouldn't make you half of a power couple. You had to be young, built, successful. A nice personality was less important than having good drugs. You had to have an opinion about Sondheim.

Now you had to have children, the highest status symbol. Straights tolerated you more if you were married and pretended to be faithful and paid high tuitions and for private riding lessons.

Of course Aldwych had none of these characteristics. Nor did August, who'd scarcely been touched by New York gay culture. He never went to Fire Island or even a gay bar. The only *barre* he knew was the one he held in ballet class. He'd hooked up a few times on Tinder, but he never saw a man twice until he met Pablo. Gay men liked him because he was beautiful and a star, though unfortunately a bottom.

August was a pure soul, as pure as a boy soprano's voice. He was serious and tireless, talented and modest. He was a good Catholic and once told Aldwych he thought of dancing as praying. He dedicated every performance to God. He went to church only at Christmas and Easter because he felt every time onstage that he was already in "church," saluting the deity. He had no opinions about Sondheim and didn't even know who he was. He revered Tchaikovsky and agreed with Baryshnikov that every dancer should bless his name, since he'd given ballet its greatest scores and had elevated it to one of the leading arts. Stravinsky was also great.

There was no doubt that August's Catholicism and his shame over his homosexuality had led him away from Aldwych's caressing hands and into Ernestine's claws. She had restored him to heterosexuality, though of a cut-rate, pitiful sort. What he now endured in bed out of a sense of duty he'd once enjoyed with an exhilarating, bright red stain of shame, an instinct, not an obligation. Now he would go to a joyless heaven where all those dimwit angels were riding around endlessly on gaudy parade floats, throwing cheap beads at the saved.

The two times Aldwych missed his August the most was when taking a shower (and having to deal with the painful disappointment of his own grotesque body) and in bed late at night (when he missed the boy's rancid breath and beautiful, sculpted body spooning his). His body was always two degrees warmer than Aldwych's, maybe because it was fifty years closer to that kiln, the womb. He would get so lonely he would cry, then get mad at himself for crying, then swear angrily he'd never waste another tear on that boy, then cry harder. Not knowing where he was living and not being able to telephone him—those were the cruelest deprivations.

One night he dreamed he rushed to the window and saw August driving by in a red convertible; August smiled and waved. The scent of this dream lingered with him all day; it was as beguiling as seeing the beautiful face of a violinist in a symphony orchestra of beards, braids, and balding men. Most nights he looked at old videos of August dancing; Aldwych kept studying them, searching for signs of weakness in the boy's leg, but never saw any.

He couldn't ask his chauffeur to drive him out to the address Warburton had given him—that would make Roger an accomplice, poor thing. Aldwych would have to rent a car, but he hadn't driven a car in twenty years. You couldn't exactly hire an Uber to drive you to the scaffold. No, he'd have to do it alone. Maybe he could take an Uber out to a car rental in the suburbs, away from the traffic. What was he afraid of? He did intend to kill himself, didn't he, after he killed the perfidious lovers?

But not before.

Aldwych wondered whether his life would have been better if he'd become a Buddhist monk (one night he saw a documentary on TV of young crew-cut monks sweeping snow off steps). But he might have broken his vows.

Aldwych loved August and hated him. The love welled up as tears, the hatred as a pugnacious chin, an "I'll-show-you" jaw. He was shocked that August didn't miss him; that must mean he was never really attached. Aldwych had been convinced that he'd tied August up in filaments of gratitude—his free room, his bed sharing, the Biarritz ballet, his kindness to Marthe (what Aldwych didn't know is that both he and Ernestine were sending her a small monthly check). Marthe didn't tell her patrons about each other, of course, of the double mensuality (nor did she tell her husband), though now, mysteriously, she dressed better and put better food on the table—better and more. Both she and her husband were getting trimmer (less starch, more protein). They told their relatives that August had a beautiful girlfriend, Anglo alas, Protestant but a real dear. That he had stopped dancing didn't bother any of the relatives. It had been an embarrassing sissy job, anyway, *n'est-ce pas*?

The Dietrich ballet came with spring to New York and received respectful reviews, but no one knew what it was and the house was rarely more than half full except on Saturday evenings. The French consul gave a dinner; the French bookstore Albertine had a signing for a book about the company, attended by only a few tiresome retired ballerinas who hadn't seen the performances but wanted to talk of their own long-forgotten careers.

Aldwych had gone only to the opening night. There was a new ballet about Lacan and "the mirror stage" of infant development with lots of big revolving mirrors. The *New Yorker* devoted a long essay to that, which was mainly about Lacan and the journalist's unsuccessful analysis. The writer was apparently homosexual, and homosexuals bored Lacan. The "hour" was only ever twenty minutes long, but Lacan often pretended this gay patient had had an important insight after just five minutes and would dismiss him at that moment of high drama so the client could meditate on it. Aldwych thought this peculiar "review" might inspire the sale of seats, but it didn't— only a lengthy exchange of heated hateful anonymous messages on Facebook.

Dietrich was astonished by Aldwych's indifference and obvious depression. The slow attendance he blamed on Aldwych's failure to hire a press agent. He knew his

dancers were performing brilliantly and he was confident of his own choreography, an antidote to the dreary
mooning of Balanchine (they said he had been a frustrated
muff diver) and the circus pyrotechnics of American
Ballet Theatre. Most of all, his company was an electri-
fying alternative to the sheer mindlessness of American
dance. The Balanchine girls were long-legged (as
well they might be, given their founder's predilections),
everything was done at an amphetamine-driven speed,
but there was no intellectual *défi* (which even in English
he preferred to say because it sounded like "defiance"
and not the correct but dull translation, "challenge").

The most important dance critic, Howard Marks, criticized the Biarritz company for its strong points—its
heavy male presence and the costumes with their prominent *nervures*. Nor did he like the original movements
invented by Dietrich. He preferred, predictably,
Balanchine's worship of Woman, his classic tutus, and his
variations on Petipa steps. He didn't seem to know who
Lacan was and attributed mirrors to a kitschy flaw in
"European" taste, because Maurice Béjart, the worst
choreographer in history, had used a mirror in a dance—a
huge one (very tacky).

. . .

August wanted to go to see the ballet.
Ernestine: No, we're not doing that.
August: Why not?

Ernestine: Because you're my slave and I say we're not going.

August: I may be your slave in the bedroom, but I'm free to do what I want in regular life.

Ernestine: (with a smile) We'll see about that. I want a full-time slave. (She gets up, crosses, tweaks his nipples and knees him in the crotch.)

August: (wincing) I know I'm your property and I love that—all your attention is on me. And I don't have to make any decisions. But honestly one last request— please, I beg of you, let me go into the city and see the Dietrich ballet.

Ernestine: But you might run into Aldwych. Or is that your plan?

August: I don't have a plan except to serve you.

Ernestine: You expect me to drive you in and see that ballet? I hate ballet. It bores me.

August: It does? (pause) Maybe you could see a movie.

Ernestine: Maybe you could start fucking obeying me. (August sobs and looks around in a panic, as if plotting his escape.) Okay, crybaby. I'll drive you in and we can watch that fucking shit. (smiling) But you have to do something for me.

August: Anything.

Ernestine: You have to wear a chastity cage around your cock and a locked stainless steel butt plug.

August: Gladly. But why?

Ernestine: (slapping him) Gladly is not the right response. It's "Yes, mistress."

August: Yes, mistress. (He lowers his head) But why all the . . . equipment?

Ernestine: I want to make sure my property is safe and can't be possessed by any other man. Usually I'd just use a chastity cage around your cock, but given what a bottom you are I want to protect your ass too. I must be the only one who has access to it.

August: I understand. Thank you. But you'll be with me the whole time.

Ernestine: Not when you go to take a leak. I want the other gays who might sneak a peek at your dick as you stand at the urinal to see the bright metal cage you're wearing. That way they'll know you're a slave. A freak.

August: Can I piss with it on?

Ernestine: Yes, you can urinate. But you can't get an erection or jerk off. Unfortunately you can't take a shit unless I unlock you. You'll just have to hold it in till we get back to the house. I may keep it in so that you'll have to ask my permission every time baby wants to poop. That gives me another idea: You should be in diapers around the house.

August: (wincing) That would be so humiliating.

Ernestine: (smiling) Yes.

She showed him the two pieces of equipment and put them on him. First she applied the cock cage, which consisted of several linked metal rings that tightened around the scrotum and locked. The other rings encased the length of his penis. "We may have to shave away all that pubic hair—it gets in the way."

"Thank you, mistress."

"Now we'll insert this aluminum butt plug."

"What if I'm not clean back there."

"So what?"

She lubricated the bulb of the plug and pushed it into his anus. She'd positioned a mirror so he could see what she was doing. She inserted a heavy, squared-off key into the near, presenting surface of the plug and turned it. Four little metal phalanges expanded inside his body; he was completely stoppered. No one would be able to fuck him, to pull him into a stall at the ballet and rape him.

"Let's leave them in just a half hour so you can get used to them. Would you feel safer with a diaper on? I think you would." He was shirtless and pantless now, just the metal gleaming around his cock and protruding slightly from his ass. She laid a pair of Pampers on the bed and pushed him back until he was lying on them. She sprinkled some sweet-smelling talcum powder on the cock and ass; she had pushed his legs back till they were raised. Then she settled him back on the diaper and fastened the sticky waistband and the leg holes. "There, now. Is baby comfortable? You're in my power, completely in my power, even your insides. Baby can take his nap now knowing his parent has taken complete control over him. Remember, you're a baby, you can't talk, all you can do is smile and laugh and coo. Let me hear you cooing."

Something in August relaxed as if he were just one great muscle untensing. He began to coo, awkwardly, in a strange voice, that shifted from falsetto to his ordinary baritone. He knew only to say *Coo, coo,* over and over again, but surely that wasn't right. He could feel the chastity cage biting into his cock as it swelled in recognition of Ernestine's total dominance. He could feel the butt plug under his diapers and he thought that if he peed or pooped it would only be normal for a little baby like him. Ernestine was twisting his nipples and his cock rose in excitement, then deflated in pain. He kept cooing and thought of the ruined, humiliated professor in *The Blue Angel* crowing obediently, ordered on by Marlene Dietrich. He said, "Don't touch my hair," and Ernestine slapped him. He ejaculated. Ernestine said, "Never saw a guy cum through a soft cock before."

Ernestine bought him a slave collar, black leather with metal studs. She put it around his neck, then attached a chain to a link and led him around. With the butt plug and cock cage, he walked with some difficulty. They watched an S&M movie, but she had the feeling August didn't want to be part of a scene.

She thought it would be fun to see Pablo fucking August. Obviously she'd liberate his hole but keep the cock cage in place.

She called Pablo on his cell and asked him if he'd like to come out to the house "for fun and games." She said she'd send a car for him.

"What's in it for me?" Pablo asked.

"I can double your massage fee."

"Okay."

She gave him the address and they agreed on a time and day. She'd send him someone from a car service she often used. She swore him to secrecy. Aldwych must not at any cost find out what their address was. Ernestine would never forgive Pablo or ever see him again if he disclosed where they were living. And she meant it!

Pablo duly came out and they all drank tea and ate crustless chicken sandwiches. After a while Ernestine left the room and came back in a black leather bustier, a whip in hand, her plentiful bush exposed. She ordered August to strip. "But no, please, I'm embarrassed." She cracked her whip and said, "You know what happens if you say no to me."

"What happens?" Pablo asked, mystified but getting visibly hard.

Blushing bright red, August removed his clothes, revealing his diaper.

Pablo exclaimed, "Coño! What's happened to you?"

Ernestine said, "If you're going to cry, start sucking on your pacifier." She stuck the rubber nipple in his mouth. "Take off your diaper and show Señor Pablo what you have in your cunt and on your clit."

The tears flowed down August's face as he tore off his diaper with three Velcro sounds.

Pablo said, "Damn! You're one sorry-ass dude." Dramatically stroking his chin as if taking inventory, Pablo slowly circled the naked, weeping August. "What have we here?" he jiggled the cock cage and looked to Ernestine for an answer.

Ernestine: It keeps him chaste. *Casta* as in *casta diva.* No sex.

Pablo frowned. He looked at August's ass and jiggled the silver end of the butt plug. "And this?"

"So no one can get in his ass, I have the key. But I'll open it for you."

"Coño!" he said again. "I don't know—his ass isn't as meaty as it was."

"We should say 'its' ass because he's an *it* now."

"But what happened?"

"It stopped dancing and its ass lost its roundness. It's pretty pathetic."

"But he can hear us, can't he? I mean 'it.' So why are you saying all these mean things out loud? You could hurt his feelings."

"It doesn't have any feelings."

"The dude is crying, in case you didn't notice, bitch."

"Is its ass too ugly to fuck now?"

"No," Pablo said.

"I'd like to see you fuck it," Ernestine said. "It can drink my piss while you fuck it."

Ernestine removed the butt plug but not the cock cage. She ordered August to go to the toilet and douche for the nice man, to throw away his dirty diaper and bring a clean one back.

"You're infernal," Pablo said to her, and she laughed.

August thought he wouldn't mind dying. The thought of death made him remember he was alone. All of us are alone in death. But didn't he want someone to hold his hand as he died? He'd been so stupid to leave his kind, protective, undemanding Aldwych. Okay, he wasn't "hot," but neither was August now, with his little belly, sagging ass and tits, his sickly emaciated face, his caged humiliated cock, his bad withered leg—he was pathetic. August had thought it would be sexy as a masochist to be desired for one's flaws, but it wasn't. It was unbearable in this "leftover life to kill," according to that book title he'd been intrigued by. He'd heard of a slave who'd killed his brutal master, then killed himself, and that was a tit-for-tat (*"berger à bergère"* in French) he understood. Since Ernestine had forbidden him to speak but only coo, his inner thoughts were entirely in his bad French. He'd forgotten English and wondered if he could still speak it if he had to. If there were a fire, or if Ernestine, for instance, was having a heart attack, would he be able to call for help?

When he returned to the bedroom after his douche and his shower, Pablo was fucking Ernestine in her vagina.

Neither of them looked to be enjoying it. Pablo pulled out of Ernestine, who snapped her fingers and ordered August to take her place. "First," she said, "suck Pablo's cock. You like that taste of pussy."

He sucked but couldn't taste anything except the strawberry-flavored lubricant. His own penis swelled in its cage and then deflated in defeat. Because he was Ernestine's slave, he felt he wasn't returned to his hateful condition as a homosexual; he was simply obeying her orders and being cuckolded as a faithful slave. Soon Pablo was fucking him as August was lying facedown except his face was planted between Ernestine's legs and she was urinating and shouting, "Swallow it!"

Pablo was so repulsed by what was happening that he lost his erection, which had never happened to him before. Impotence made him so angry that he stood up and said, "You two are really sick! I had no idea you'd gone so far, so far down." He pulled his jeans up and buttoned them and headed out the door to the waiting car she'd arranged. He didn't close the A-frame door behind him. It was a foggy late spring day—mist was rising off the lake. For a moment Ernestine was taken aback, but she rushed to the door in her black corset and shouted, "Your money! I haven't paid you yet."

Pablo said, "Fuck that! I'm outta here."

Ernestine warned, "No giving our address away to Aldwych."

Pablo, getting into the car, called out, "Fuck you! Fuck you both. I do what I want."

The car drove away.

· · ·

Ernestine had a moment of doubt about her whole existence. She looked at the pitiful August kneeling at her feet, his shiny cock cage gleaming in the late sunlight, his face and hair wet from her piss, and she thought, *Is this what I've created? Have I turned a divo into a whimpering slave?* She looked at his shaved pubes, his grotesquely deflated ass, his scarred leg, and mused that not even his own mother would recognize him now. Pablo's contempt rang in her ears. She had lost every guarantee that he wouldn't reveal their whereabouts to Aldwych. Would the angry old man—ruined, robbed, betrayed—come out to their A-frame and denounce them?

She had always obeyed her own whims and was rich enough, powerful enough to be able to fulfill them. Her desires had always pleased her, but now they looked shoddy. This poor ex-dancer had lost his athletic body, and his mouth would soon be smeared with her poop.

Before their ballet evening she cleaned him up, helped him into his suit, and fastened his cufflinks. She kept his asshole free of the locked diaphragm but did not remove the cock cage. If he was attracted to the dancers or if someone cruised him at the urinal he'd suffer a bit from "a Hollywood half-loaf" (the beginning of tumescence) and remember his mistress.

. . .

In the car they barely spoke, and she tuned in Ravel's first important composition, *Pavane for a Dead Princess*. When she looked at August's face in the dull late sunlight, he appeared diminished, extinct. Had he lost weight? She must weigh him. Was he ill? Or sick unto death? Maybe the ballet would cheer him up, bring back some of his old fight—or better, show him the futility of excellence in dance.

The house was only half full, which brought a little smile to August's lips (only the beginning of a smile). He looked around the auditorium with a blink of recognition and surprise—he'd rarely seen it in full light. It really was the height of sixties ugliness. A little lady going down the aisle stopped and turned her whole body toward him, as if her neck were too stiff to move. She studied him for a moment too long and at last asked in a whisper, "August Dupond?"

August said politely, "No. People often make that mistake. Who was he?"

"A very great dancer. Much younger than you. Now that I look, I see you are nothing like him. You look like a car wreck." She smiled as if she'd cracked a joke and continued down the aisle. August thought she must be a very great lady. He was relieved that he slightly resembled the dancer but not too closely.

Finally the last stragglers rushed in. The audience was still very thin, and many people moved down from the balconies to the empty seats closer to the stage. The orchestra tuned up, the scariest moment for any performer. Some dancers, he remembered, even made the sign of the cross and kissed their thumbs backstage. The girls were rubbing their toe shoes in the rosin box. They all took their places onstage. The orchestra played the familiar overture. The brilliant stage lights came on. The curtain whispered up and random audience members (the patrons, no doubt, or tourists) applauded the opening tableau—the seamless blue backdrop and the buff-colored leotards and tops.

August was impressed by the dancing, the innovative choreography, and the steps, but he thought the women were not as fast and accurate as Balanchine's. The men were excellent but none as good as August had been before his accident.

At the first intermission he went to the toilet because he knew Ernestine would want to hear all about it. He stood in line waiting for an opening at the urinal. A place opened and he stood next to a wide-shouldered man whose long graying hair was held back in a pony-tail. The men on his right and left didn't look at his imprisoned penis. It took him so long to urinate that he became embarrassed and looked up at the plastered ceiling; finally the flow came.

When he returned to his seat Ernestine gave him a thumbs-up, which he resented. During the next dance she held her hand on his knee on the crippled side. A pianist played a fughetto by Bach, as the program said. When August looked at the mechanical puppet-like movements of the all-male cast, August remembered Balanchine's beautiful *Concerto Barocco*, with its deep understanding of the music. Dietrich was just choreographing the trills.

August felt contented that willy-nilly he'd remained faithful to the great Balanchine. The men rushed offstage and an undertrained ballerina trembled through her leg extensions as the pianist played (as he saw from the program) the heartbreakingly beautiful adagio from the organ sonata no. 4 BWV528 transcribed by August Stradal. Was it their shared first name or the great, unfamiliar music, or the dancer's obviously unrewarded efforts?—or the combination? August burst into silent tears, which bathed his face. Ernestine didn't notice, thankfully. Most of the time he felt relieved, solaced to be free of the self, of himself, and to be her property. No more decisions, no more limits, no more scrambling after goals; and at least she was a woman and he was no longer cursed with homosexuality.

But at other times he felt desperate, as if he were sinking in quicksand and there was no one to rescue him; though his submersion was slow and gradual, he could see no future except in a mineral death by drowning. He called out as loudly as he could, he struggled to keep his arms above the sinkhole and to cast his hands side to side, but his screams were ignored in the roaring silence and his fingers could never stretch that far. He knew he was going to die and he tried not to care. There was a short supply of panic that fought against his demise, but if he drew a deep breath he had to recognize it wouldn't matter—certainly not to the public except for a few old men drooling over his yellowing performance photographs, his powerful legs and mouthwatering buttocks, his plentifully stuffed codpiece. His mother would be consoled by Ernestine—and would profit from her sympathy. His father would shrug, eternally puzzled by his offspring. Maybe Zaza and Aldwych would be the only ones to care. He himself would be glad to be free of this torment called life, something that hadn't really worked out. He remembered his kindly catechism teacher who had said he believed in hell because it was canonical, but he was convinced there was no one in it. In any event he had repented of his mortal sin, homosexuality, and redeemed himself.

The most he could expect from Ernestine was a shrug.

But why was he so certain his death was imminent?

He feared it in truth, but he feared not dying more. Years ago, after he'd first fooled around with a man (and well before he knew about the antivirals), he'd meditated one afternoon in a clearing in the woods and asked his body if he was going to die of AIDS. And his body had whispered *No*.

But now it was saying *Yes*.

18

Pablo told Aldwych about the "sterile" house and the spring-muddy lawn surrounding it. "Sterile" was such a surprising word for Pablo to use that it reverberated in Aldwych's mind and seemed to have a greater, sinister import.

He gave Aldwych the address. He described August's pitiful state and his genital attachments and Ernestine's cruelty and bustier and urination. Aldwych was so grateful to Pablo that he went down on Pablo that night in bed, something he usually avoided, since Pablo was not August. He couldn't truly desire anyone else, and the few times he'd surrendered to Pablo he'd felt like an adulterer. Pablo behaved like Caliban, whereas Aldwych wanted only his Ariel, graceful and shy.

That evening he wrote a note to Laurence Butterfield:

Dear Laurence, By the time you get this I will have murdered two people and killed myself. You might want to send the coroner or an ambulance or hearse, whatever you think is appropriate, to this address: 41 Lilac Lane ("Mon Plaisir"). The woman is my cousin Ernestine, and you might return her corpse to her husband, Bryce Masters, at 41 Beekman, apartment 4. He might choose to bury her on her father's estate, though I don't know if an interment is legal on private property in New Jersey. Nor is it any of my business.

I've bought a double lot for August Dupond and me in a mausoleum in Short Hills, the leading death industry in New Jersey at Memorial Properties. We will want a Catholic ceremony (no wake) in respect to August's faith. I have prepaid all funeral expenses and include here the receipt; I have itemized embalming fees, clergy fees, ground covering, etc., but there should be enough funds after the sale of the Saugatuck cottage to meet any unexpected charges. Please contact the deceased's mother, Marthe Vielleville, by phone to notify her of her son's disappearance, but only after the funeral. Her number is 817 294 7786. A French speaker might be necessary. I've left her a small bequest. You must ask her for her banking details.

The whole tragedy might end in farce, as so often in my life, if Ernestine manages to disarm me and kills me first. If I'm the only cadaver, bury me in a single plot in Short Hills and give the refund to August, if he is still alive and sane.

You might imagine that my actions are based on financial disappointment, but rest assured they are inspired only by unrequited love.

Sincerely, Aldwych West

At first Aldwych was nervous about driving his rented Honda, a reaction he thought of as illustrative—the fear of dying en route to one's own death. Once he was in the country he calmed down and found some consolation in his very ability to drive. He turned on the radio, then immediately switched it off in deference to these last solemn moments of his life.

His plan was to enter the room and brandish his Glock. He would fire at once into August's bad leg—to frighten them both and to demonstrate how pitiless he was—to injure this poor leg August had spent months trying to rehabilitate.

But what if they weren't in the living room?

He'd round them up at gunpoint, both of them groggy from napping.

Then he'd order Ernestine to unlock the penis cage and the butt plug. He didn't want August to lie beside him for eternity with her hardware in him.

Ernestine in an uncharacteristic moment would beg him to kill her but spare August, who would instantly object. "Why would I want to live without you?"

"Don't be silly, August."

He would shoot Ernestine and let her writhe and bubble her way into a slow death as August held his bleeding leg and sobbed.

Then, after August had taken in the whole agony, Aldwych would press his head to August, ear to ear, and fire his gun. No, he would shoot August first, then himself, in case his cranium deflected the bullet.

· · ·

The next morning, when the maid, holding fresh flowers, let herself in at ten on a sunny day, she found three corpses, two of them slumped together. She screamed and called the police.

ACKNOWLEDGMENTS

Thanks to my wonderful editor, Daniel Loedel—thorough, a great writer, an excellent editor. To Emily DeHuff and Jasmine Kwityn, who copyedited and proofread my manuscript and who saved me from many, many mistakes. To Bill Clegg, my ideal agent (who is also an important writer). To John McManus, an accomplished novelist, who accompanied me through every hard-won page. To Yi-Yun Li, my Eglantine.

And to my intelligent, resourceful husband, loving companion, beautiful writer, and a true master of plotting, Michael Carroll.

A NOTE ON THE AUTHOR

EDMUND WHITE is the author of many novels, including *A Boy's Own Story*, *The Beautiful Room Is Empty*, *The Farewell Symphony*, *Our Young Man*, *A Saint from Texas*, and *A Precious Life*. His nonfiction includes *City Boy*, *Inside a Pearl*, *The Unpunished Vice*, and other memoirs; *The Flâneur*, about Paris; and literary biographies and essays. He was the 2018 winner of the PEN/Saul Bellow Award for Achievement in American Fiction and received the 2019 Medal for Distinguished Contribution to American Letters from the National Book Foundation.